HANGFIRE

HANGFIRE

JOHN H. MATTHEWS

BLUEBULLSEYE PRESS

HANGFIRE
Written by John H. Matthews
©2019 John H. Matthews

ISBN: 978-1-970071-03-0

Library of Congress Control Number: 2019905442

Bluebullseye Press
A division of Bluebullseye LLC

Edited by Shea Megale

Cover design ©2019 John H. Matthews

Also by John H. Matthews

The South Coast

Ballyvaughan

Designated Survivor

Red Grace: A Grace Short Story

Family Line

For Brennan,

You are my favorite person on this planet,
and always will be.

CHAPTER 1

The padlock snapped closed and Clem Akins slid the small silver key into the side pocket of his lightweight olive tactical pants. His hand moved up and rested on the grip of the FNS-9 pistol at his hip, to him a reflexive motion no different than making sure your car keys are in your pocket.

He climbed into the base model Chevy Impala rented with a stolen credit card and license. Drastic measures, he'd told himself, as he lifted the wallet from the inebriated man having drinks at a Chili's bar with co-workers an hour earlier. By the time the man was sober enough to realize his wallet was gone, it would be in the Colorado River, credit cards and all.

It wasn't without guilt. He'd watched his target drinking for half an hour and told himself that his friends would cover his bar tab and help him get home. It was the third bar he'd visited looking for someone whose driver's license would pass light enough scrutiny to use from an underpaid car rental agency clerk. The photo of the African American man on the ID looked enough like him. Using his own card and identification wasn't an option. He would be tracked too quickly.

Clem's training and career as an Army Ranger prepared him for the unexpected, for evading an enemy while always looking for a way to attack, and staying alive while doing it. Stealing wallets was something he'd learned as a teenager in Oak Cliff, southwest of Dallas, as a means of survival before joining the Army. The judge had said jail or Army, so he signed up and was shipped to Fort Benning to learn what real sweat was in the humid Georgia summer. He'd decided with a forty-pound pack on his back on a twenty-mile run that he wouldn't screw up again. He would be a lifer in the Army, and that he'd be good at it. His record from the juvenile court was sealed and he left Oak Cliff behind him for good.

He drove away from the self-storage park, his daily driver Korean War era Army Jeep locked inside, and headed toward the river to dispose of the wallet then figure out his next move. His Jeep was the opposite of subtle and would paint a bullseye on him. He had to hide it. The rental blended in with the tourists, unmarked police, and state vehicles from the capitol building, granting him basic camouflage.

This wasn't what he'd expected from his Friday night. Usually he'd be watching television in his small house while cleaning one of his weapons, which was exactly what he had been doing until five hours earlier when a barrage of bullets blasted through the walls of his small home from four masked assailants. He'd taken two down before the others pulled the limp bodies into a large black SUV and sped away. It was less than ten minutes later that he left the house without knowing if he'd ever return. Instead he had a survivalist backpack in the trunk and enough ammunition to wage a small war while driving a rented car with a radio that wouldn't even hold a station without turning to static every few seconds.

It wasn't his doing. A mistake made years earlier came back, something he thought was behind him and forgotten. But bad people don't just go away that easily, he learned. It had only been the catalyst, an opening to a world he'd heard of but had nothing to do with, actions that would get you imprisoned or killed.

He needed help and he knew it. This was different than creating a battle plan and leading his men into combat. This was covert operations, reconnaissance, and information gathering. This was what his friend Eddie Holland did, not him. Details couldn't be left behind for just anyone to find, it had to be subtle, clues that most would overlook. He'd left a breadcrumb already and in a few hours would strike the first spark to get his friend in action, hoping he would understand and follow the trail.

But now, he just needed to disappear.

CHAPTER 2

The pain crept up my arm. My shoulder burned. I opened my eyes and stared at the alabaster white ceiling where I was trapped. Or was it eggshell. A slight move and another flash of pain from my joint being twisted beyond its natural limits brought me back from contemplating shades of white and instead I began to consider my options for escape. It was cold in the room and I felt exposed in nothing but my green boxers, all my other clothes having been torn off of me. I didn't plan on dying here.

It had been more than an hour in this position and my patience was worn. I raised my head to assess my captor. Eyes were closed, likely asleep. Amateur. It was either now or I wait until my arm shriveled up and died. I knew I would regret it and the consequences of my actions would be extreme if caught, but the only other option was chewing my arm off, which was impractical. I'd been held captive before and waiting for backup never works. There was nobody that knew I was here, that I needed help.

I adjusted my body, boxer shorts twisting and pinching delicate skin as I did, and began to pull my arm out. The blood rushing to long deserted arteries felt like hot water being poured over my skin and I had to bite my tongue to keep from laughing, crying, and screaming out at the same time. At the halfway point, I looked over for signs of life again, eyes still closed. The door was across the room. I knew it was unlocked. If I acted quickly, I could be free and out before retaliation. I yanked and my arm was free, but the tingling stung. Before I could even rub my aching shoulder, a hand came up and slapped my bare chest.

Her eyes were wide open and glaring at me. "What the hell, Eddie!" She rolled over with her back to me and was asleep again.

The night before had ended with us more than a bit drunk and making love in three different rooms of the house. We'd collapsed into bed well after midnight. I don't know arm ended up under her, but damage was done and I was free. And I was hungry. After pulling on a T-shirt from the floor beside our bed, I went downstairs to make scrambled eggs.

A free day was rare. Either Eva had to work the emergency room or I was exhausted from being at my bar for a concert the night before. I'd looked forward to today all week and hoped to spend most of it right back in bed once she'd woken up and we'd both brushed our teeth.

We'd moved in together almost a year earlier. Most of my belongings were still in boxes in various parts of the house.

I did have drawers in the dresser and a few inches of space in the closet, but since my wardrobe consisted mostly of T-shirts, jeans, and hats, I didn't need much room. I had never lived with anyone, except for the bunks at Quantico for sixteen weeks where I shared a room with my oldest friend Gus.

I sat at the high-top counter and ate my eggs and toast. I had no newspaper to read and considered turning the television, but decided against the inane banter of overpaid celebrities and just stared into nothing and enjoyed my food. Current events were not my strong suit. I checked my phone and saw one text from my sister wanting me to call her.

It was another hour before Eva woke and came down the stairs. I could only stare with a schoolboy grin as she stopped on the last step and rubbed her eyes, then did a full body stretch, arms over her head, like she was in a coffee commercial. A very sexy coffee commercial. My old blue button-down shirt she'd found in my boxes was loose on her body and as she stretched it raised up above her violet La Perla panties. Oh, how I loved those panties.

She crossed the room and wrapped her arms around me, then reached her face up for a kiss. Even her morning breath seemed cute. I'd found nothing wrong with her, or nothing I would accept as being wrong, just effortless beauty. When I'd reach my hand down and stroke her thigh, she complained that she hadn't shaved and I couldn't feel anything but the smoothness of her light brown skin. On days we were off together she'd throw on jeans, a loose fitting v-neck tee, and a ball cap and I couldn't stop staring at her. I would tell her how gorgeous she was and she'd give me that roll with her big brown eyes then squeeze my face and tell me I'm cute and blind.

"Make any eggs for me?"

I glanced at the dirty frying pan in the sink. "Uhh, no. Didn't know how late you'd sleep."

She put on her best sad puppy dog face. "Would you, please?" The please was dragged out until I relented and turned to rinse the frying pan and make her breakfast.

"So you're still off today?"

"Sure am," Eva said.

"A whole day together? Whatever will we do?"

"I have a few ideas."

I smiled. "I bet you do."

"There's a new antique shop in Round Rock I want to go to."

"Not really what I was thinking." I cracked two eggs over the medium hot pan and a splash of olive oil.

"I know what you were thinking," she said. "I always know what you're thinking."

"Am I that transparent?"

"No. You're that horny."

I stopped and looked across the room at nothing in particular as if in deep thought. "That's true. I really am."

She threw a dish towel at me to break my introspection. "Nothing on your schedule for the weekend then?"

"Just you. I have a show at the club tomorrow night I need to stop by for, but we could make it a date." I'd bought Buddy's Music Saloon with Gus over a year ago after a case ended in Buddy being shot in his own club. We had live music at least four nights a week and kept the doors closed when no bands were booked.

"Aww." She wrapped her arms around me. "That's sad."

"Damn. I was going for pathetic."

"You almost had it."

After she'd finished breakfast, I worked my best moves of seduction and fortunately for me, her resistance was low. We didn't even make it all the way to the bedroom, finding ourselves on the landing halfway up the stairs, naked and entwined. It wasn't comfortable but it was good.

Once we had collapsed into post-coitus exhaustion and relaxed for a few minutes, she announced she was going to take a long shower and take her time getting ready since there was no rush today. I understood this to mean I had at least two hours before we'd be going anywhere, so I pulled on my shorts, blue and silver Brooks running shoes, a loose fitting tank top, and headed out for a run.

I missed running from my old apartment just outside of downtown Austin. My route would take me along Lady Bird Lake Trail, through Zilker Park, unless it was one of the festival weekends full of annoying tourists who come and buy Keep Austin Weird T-shirts then go home feeling like they were suddenly hip, and over into the city if I felt like it. From Eva's house, our house, it was residential rolling hills and avoiding being hit by Escalades driving 65 in a 40 zone.

The straight stretches of road were at least easier for endurance training, slowing my pace to nearly a walk then sprinting when my watch beeped to tell me it was time for a two-minute sprint. I put in nearly ten miles before returning back to the house only to find Eva still wrapped in her post-shower towel while sitting on the bed reading a magazine.

We took her car since she hated my truck so there wasn't much of a debate. She found a parking space facing the water tower and we walked into the small downtown of Round Rock. We stopped halfway for caffeine and she had a croissant with her latte while I people-watched and sipped an iced coffee, trying my hardest to look manly doing so.

Conversation was always easy with Eva. Comfortable. We'd had a violent start to our relationship. Our first date ended with an intruder in her home there to lure me in to kill me. He failed. I'd held her until the ambulance came and I haven't stopped holding her since.

"So you wanting to buy some antiques today?"

"No. I just like looking," she said.

A woman walked by with a dog the size of a rat on a leash, a cellphone to her ear and talking loudly about how cute the dog was.

"Are we doomed as a civilization?" I pondered.

Eva thought for a moment. "I don't think so. At some point smart has to win out over stupid."

"I hope you're right."

My phone vibrated in the pocket of my shorts. I pulled it out and glanced at the screen.

"Who is it?" she said. "One of your other women?"

"You're the only woman for me, sweet cheeks. It's a text from Clem."

"That's rare."

"It is." I unlocked the phone and tapped in to read the message. Then I read it again.

"You look confused."

"More so than usual?"

"Slightly," she said. "What did he say?"

"Says he's going on vacation and asked if I'd feed his fish every couple days."

"That's a long drive to feed someone's fish, even Clem's."

"He doesn't have fish. Hates them. Sees no point unless they can be eaten."

Her attention came fully to me. "Then why did he ask you?"

I stared out across the street as a large truck drove past, the sound and vibration stopping everyone's conversations for a moment, made even worse by the thundering bass coming out the open windows. "I don't know, but I think I gotta go find out."

Moments later I was off the phone with Gus and twenty minutes after that I was kissing Eva goodbye in the middle of the sidewalk, my hands moving down her back as tongues swirled together in unholy matrimony until she finally pushed me away before I could grab her ass in front of everyone.

"Go. Get out of here," she said. "But come back soon because I need more of that."

CHAPTER 3

The black Ford Explorer blocked a whole lane of traffic. Cars stopped behind it, waiting. There were emergency lights mounted in the grill, inside at the top of the windshield, flashing markers on the sides, and four more in the rear window. As I walked up to the truck he turned them all on. The windows were tinted limo black.

I opened the door and climbed in. "Very discreet."

"Yeah. Like a sledgehammer," Gus said. "People see me coming up behind them on the highway and almost crash to get out of the way, and that's without turning on my lights."

"Is that a complaint?"

"No," he said. "I love it."

We never shake hands or hug or even greet each other, we simply pick up where we left off. We've known each other since our ages were in single digits. From grade school to second-string high school football to the FBI academy at Quantico, and even now in my post-FBI detective jobs, we're never too far away from each other. He's now in charge of the Austin satellite field office for the bureau and I heavily abuse him and his resources whenever I can. He complains about it but I know he enjoys it, too.

"Where to?" he said.

"Maxdale."

"Where the hell is Maxdale?"

"It's a bump on the road southwest of Killeen."

"Of course it is."

A few minutes later he was merging the large SUV onto I-35 headed north and settled into the left lane at 85 mph. I'd left the FBI after years of counterterrorism and had come home to Austin. Private detective jobs kept me busy and the bar even more so. The bureau kept me on speed dial and I helped out as I could, which meant occasional trips to D.C. on short notice.

"So what's the story?"

"There isn't much of a story yet." I gave him what little information I had and he just looked over at me and back to the road.

"His fish?"

"Yup."

"So we're speeding up there because he asked you to take care of his nonexistent fish?"

"Yup."

He nodded and kept driving. One thing you can count on in Texas is long, straight, flat roads. Even in the oversized vehicle, what few curves were thrown at us were easily handled and speed maintained. Once on the smaller two-lane road we easily overtook a couple of small cars without even speeding up.

Maxdale doesn't have its own post office or any real roads other than the eponymous Maxdale Road. There's no sign to announce you've entered the town or to thank you for visiting. The actual population of Maxdale is unknown but thought to be around four, and at least one of those is rumored to be a cow.

We missed the dirt road and had to turn around and go back.

"He lives here?" Gus climbed out of the SUV.

Clem's home is a long and narrow shotgun house still standing from the oil boom nearly a hundred years earlier. He'd moved it from west Texas to land he owned in Maxdale. It had probably been assigned to the oil company and housed the project foreman, the actual workers relegated to tents or whatever else they could find. Clem had done a lot of work to the house, but mostly inside. He never wanted attention drawn to the building or himself.

Gus mounted the three steps to the bare wooden porch and tried to peer in the front door. "Can't see a damn thing."

"By design."

He tried the screen door but it was latched from the inside.

"Where is he?"

"Don't know."

"How are you supposed to help him?"

I was about to answer, then didn't. I stepped up to the porch beside him and knelt down.

"What is it?" Gus said.

"Looks like a bullet hole," I said.

Gus stepped back and took in the front of the house. "There's another. And there."

Once we knew what we were looking for we found dozens of holes. The old multicolored roof siding that covered the walls of the house obscured them well, blending in to the different tones of the faded asphalt shingles. There were distinctive patterns we recognized from automatic weapons fired in three-round bursts.

I walked down the side of the house, watching the open field to my left as much as I did the ground in front of me, peeking in through the few windows. White discount store shades were pulled down and hung wider than the openings, blocking any view. More bullet holes lined the wall. The windows were intact, likely bullet resistant plexiglass lining the outside of the original frames.

Behind the house, a cement mound stuck out of the ground twenty feet from the back door, the top of the tornado shelter that had likely seen more jars of fruit preserves over the last century than people seeking safety from a storm. An old farmhouse had been on the plot of land but lost to a fire shortly before Clem bought the property. He'd cleared the debris and poured the foundation for the shotgun house himself. The low angled door to the tornado shelter was padlocked.

Gus came from the other side of the house and reached up to the back screen door.

"That one's latched from the inside, too," he said. "More holes along the other side."

"They seem to stop before getting to the back of the

house," I said. "I'm guessing three shooters, maybe four, fanned out but not getting too far from their getaway vehicle."

"And to avoid getting hit in the crossfire," Gus said.

"Very professional."

"You think he's inside, that one of those rounds clipped him?" Gus tried to look in through another window.

"I don't," I said. "Knowing him he's lined the walls behind the sheetrock with dampening material to slow down any projectiles."

"We can get one of these screen doors open easily enough but I'm guessing the door itself will be harder to crack open without really tearing into it. How do you leave your house with the screen doors latched from the inside?"

I stepped back and looked up at the roof of the house, then turned to the yard and settled my eyes on the storm cellar. I walked over to it then turned to Gus.

"You have any bolt cutters in that fancy FBI truck of yours?"

"I do, but I really don't want to get them scratched up," Gus said. "Might hurt the resale value."

"I'll be careful."

When Gus returned with the cutters, he went to the storm cellar door and placed the two large blades on either side of the loop on the steel padlock, then squeezed the handles together. The lock split and slid down the front of the metal door to the dirt.

I opened the door and stepped down into the shelter, taking the three long steps to the cement floor, and Gus followed. A string hanging from the ceiling turned on the three bare, 100 watt bulbs which lit the small white space up like a dying sun.

"Whoa," Gus said. "We sure Clem's on our side?"

One wall was covered with pistols, shotguns, and assault riles. A few empty brackets dotted the wall. The low bookshelf below the weapons held boxes of ammunition to fit all the calibers of weapons above.

"Gotta be at least a hundred weapons. Minus a few. From the sizes of the empty spots I'd say looks like a few rifles and a pair of pistols are missing."

It wasn't musty like every other storm cellar I'd been in. I couldn't see any, but it felt like conditioned air was being pumped into the small space. The cement floor was covered in a berber rug. The table and chair looked like they came from Pottery Barn.

"We should submit this place to Better Homes and Bunkers," I said.

"Check this out," Gus said. "Spaces for three backpacks under this shelf, but one is gone."

I moved around the small round room, then stopped in front of a bookcase. A few Steinbeck titles, some Stephen King, various classics, and a whole shelf of Vince Flynn novels were there. Looking down I saw a quarter-inch gap between the bottom shelf and the cement floor.

"Clem wouldn't, would he?" I felt along the edges then began moving books. When I pulled on The Count of Monte Cristo, a soft click sounded from behind the wall.

"No way," Gus said. "He built a secret room in his storm cellar?"

I swung the door open and a series of LED lights came

on down a long, narrow hallway. "And this is a tunnel, not a room."

"This explains how he got out of the house with the doors locked from the inside." Gus shook his head in disbelief.

"And why he did all the work himself," I said. "He didn't want anyone knowing what was under the house."

At the end of the tunnel was a ladder. At the top I turned around and felt the wall until my fingers found a release. The wall swung out and I stepped out of the pantry into the kitchen. Gus's head appeared as he climbed up and joined me.

"Gotta say that's pretty damn cool," he said.

"Let's look for anything out of place."

It was clean inside and minimal. There was hardly anything personal to be found. There was one photo of Clem when he met George W. Bush while in physical therapy at Walter Reed and that was about it.

After a sweep of the one-bedroom house we headed back through the tunnel. I picked up one of the backpacks and handed the other to Gus.

"What's this for?"

"Clem felt he needed to take one, so maybe we should also."

Once outside we looked at the now useless padlock.

"Can't leave all those weapons unlocked," I said.

Gus raised his hand with a finger up. "I have an idea." He turned and jogged off toward the front of the house. A minute later he returned with a pair of handcuffs and latched both through the hasp on the door and locked them tight.

"Nice thinking," I said. "I want to look around out here for a minute."

It didn't take long to find what I was looking for. Not far from the SUV was a scattering of spent shell casings. I found another thirty-feet away. Gus found two more.

"I have blood here," I said.

Gus came over and knelt down.

"Sure looks like it." He looked at the ground near the blood. "Looks like someone was dragged."

He stood and walked away from where I was standing, staring at the ground, and passed where the next closest shooting location was.

"Several sets of tire tracks here," he said. "One looks like the narrow tires from Clem's Jeep. These are ours." He pointed to tracks leading away from him. "Those are a third set. Sped off that way, then looks like it circled around through the tall grass and went left onto the road."

I looked around, feeling very exposed in the flat countryside. I had no reason to think the shooters would be back, especially in the daylight, but didn't want to take chances either.

CHAPTER 4

With the Explorer back on the road, I relaxed a bit, but kept checking the rearview mirror on the passenger side. I knew Gus noticed but he didn't say anything. Maybe it's just that I don't have my sidearm, the security blanket of law enforcement officers and two-bit private eyes. Maybe it's that I'm losing my edge, my sense of daring, my lack of regard for danger. Maybe I'm just getting old.

"Want me to drop you at home?" Gus said.

"Not yet. We need to go to Fort Hood," I said.

"Yessir."

"Keep that up and I'll give you a five-star rating," I said. "Have any bottled water? Chewing gum?"

"Screw you."

"One star now. Worst Uber ever."

It only took twenty minutes for Gus to drive us to Fort

Hood. We cleared the guard booth and wound our way through to the large building that looked like an abandoned warehouse that Clem Akins used as his training center for soldiers wishing to become Army Rangers. It was his second-chance career as an Army man after an injury most men would have retired from and spent the rest of their years fighting with the VA for medical assistance. But not Clem. He was a soldier. A Ranger. A lifer.

Clem had been the leader of a ground operation the Joint Terrorism Task Force had ordered in Afghanistan. I was part of that task force as an FBI agent in counter-terrorism and had sat in a dark room in Virginia watching satellite feeds of his men storming a remote village, only to have the primary target explode, killing several men and taking Clem's left leg off just above the knee. It hadn't been my intel that led to the raid but I still felt responsible, a voyeur in a Herman Miller chair sipping bad coffee while men died. I continued with the task force a few more months but eventually found a way to get reassigned away from the promotion-driven agency egos who cared more about racking up confirmed kills from their cubicles than the human lives those kills represented.

Many months after that failed mission, a quick search from my desk at the Washington Field Office had found Clem Akins' service record and his current location. The next day I stood at the end of the long narrow physical therapy room at Walter Reed hospital, watching the tall proud black man struggling to stand upright with the fiberglass and steel prosthetic strapped on his thigh to replace the flesh, blood and bone left on the ground in Afghanistan.

I don't think there was any protocol broken or unwritten rule that should have kept me from talking to Clem, aside from the top secret clearance level information I possessed about the operation that changed his life forever, but we never discussed the mission aside from me telling him I knew what happened, and had been involved. He never gave me a bad look or a mean word. He wasn't looking for an apology and I wasn't looking for forgiveness. Maybe I was looking for understanding. Both he and I dedicated our lives to our country, and both of us were in the line of fire. But watching the Rangers, SEALs, and other elite forces do their jobs had impressed me to no end.

It started with a cup of coffee that afternoon, drinks at a bar in Bethesda a few weeks later, and we felt like lifelong friends before he headed home to Texas. Without his knowledge, I'd made a phone call to an old friend of my father's, someone with a star on his collar and a lot of pull, to ask that Clem be kept in service. He had so much more to offer.

It wasn't much longer before I got fed up with the bureaucracy and found myself back in Austin as well, trailing cheating husbands and snapping photos of people scamming the system for disability checks.

The front door of Clem's building at Fort Hood was unlocked and I walked in, calling his name as I did, only to hear the emptiness of the giant rooms. His office was just inside the front door to the right and on his desk sat a half-full cup of cold coffee and a bare but coffee stained blotter with random notes and phone numbers scribbled on it in ballpoint pen. Nothing was out of place or jumped up and yelled "clue" at me. The desk drawers were locked as was the filing cabinet in the corner. Looking back at the desk, the edge of a white envelope was barely visible along the left side of the blotter. I slid it aside and picked up the envelope, no words or writing on it.

I tore the envelope open and pulled out the single piece of canary yellow paper and scanned it, then went back and read it thoroughly but found no more useful information than I did from the initial skimming.

The office was sparsely decorated. The grey metal desk and chair with no padding sat to one side and another pair of chairs against the other wall. No awards on the shelves or walls, not being his style to show off his achievements. His Purple Heart along with all his other medals were in a box back at his house, on the bottom shelf of a bookcase in his living room. Above his desk, a faded map of the Davis Mountains was pinned on the wall.

I left the office behind to walk the rest of the building, feeling I wouldn't be doing my detective due diligence if I didn't. I found Gus in the hallway, having just checked out the locker room and second office that sat empty of any furnishings. We walked through the double doors into a large open room. Flipping a row of switches on the wall, the lights popped on slowly high above the floor. The indoor facility had an obstacle course, a wrestling mat that had been salvaged from a high school gym being torn down in Killeen, and an enclosed live-fire scenario shooting range. Clem and I spent many hours in the range, loaded pistols in hand, waiting for whatever surprise he'd set up for me.

Gus turned his head to look around at the empty room, then down at my right hand. "What's that?"

"I guess you FBI types would call it a clue."

He took the paper from me and read it far more thoroughly than I had on my first look at it.

"It's a packing slip for a shipment to Fort Hood," he said. "For 32-pounds of tortillas."

"Is that a lot?"

"For a single guy, yes. For a Mexican restaurant, no," Gus said. "Does Clem own a Mexican restaurant?"

"Not that I know of."

"Then what's it mean?"

"Haven't figured that part out yet."

"Think it's important?"

"Don't know," I said. "It's the only thing we've found that was available for the finding. I've been in his office many times. There's usually books and binders and folders stacked up."

I'm usually optimistic in the first days of a case, even if nothing concrete is found. It's the mystery, the unknown. I loved the hunt for anything out of the ordinary. In the FBI I spent years looking for one peculiarity to stand out in thousands of documents of mostly normal things, something to pull the thread just a little bit so I could trace it across the material to the other side. That was for a greater good, the safety of the nation, our military, civilians. Here I am looking for one man who may, or may not, be in danger. Odds are good that he is. Normal people don't have bullet holes peppering their home.

After checking out the rest of the building, we went back out and stood in front of his black SUV.

"Oh-for-two," I said. "The packing slip is the only hard evidence so far. I need to figure out what it's for, and if it even has anything to do with this."

"How about Brady?" Gus said.

"Brady who?

"Brady, Texas. It's the address on the packing slip," Gus said.

CHAPTER 5

I kept pushing the scan button on the radio trying to find a station that would come in strong enough without turning to static.

"How do you not have any CD's in here?"

"First of all, it's my work car and I've only had it two weeks. Second of all, who uses CDs anymore? I keep all my music on my phone."

"On your phone? Really? Have you no respect?" I shook my head. "Is that any way to treat music?"

Gus looked left out the window, one hand on the steering wheel.

"I saw that eye roll," I said.

"What, you going to tell me the only way to listen to music is on vinyl?" Gus said.

"Not the only way. Just the best way."

"When's the last time you even played a record?"

"A few days ago," I mumbled. "Maybe last week."

"Right."

I finally landed on a station out of the University of Texas that had Spoon's Hot Thoughts playing and was followed by an old Robert Earl Keen track. I sang along and even caught Gus mouthing some of the words, fingers tapping on the steering wheel.

We'd road tripped together more times than two people should. In high school it was driving down to Galveston. In college we started hitting Padre Island and eventually New Orleans. Working cases together we'd been to Mexico and every corner of Texas. We'd get on each other's nerves, but never enough for anything to come between us.

After arriving in Brady, Texas, the GPS in the Explorer took us right to the address from the packing slip. We parked on the street and stared out the window at the old building on the west edge of town.

"A dead end dirt road. Seems redundant."

"Keeps it private," Gus said.

"Clem is ordering tortillas from here?"

"I really doubt that." Gus dialed his phone and talked when an agent answered on the other end. "Yeah, it's Gus. Need you to run a business for me." He gave the name and address from the packing slip then hung up.

"Guess we should take a look around."

"Drove all this way," he said.

Gus locked the SUV with the button on his key, the chirp of the horn as the alarm activated echoed off the side of the building. "So much for the element of surprise," he said.

"Not sure there's going to be anyone to surprise."

Rounding the corner to the front of the building, a long cement ramp ran up to the loading dock designed to handle forklifts and dollies to load and unload smaller trucks. Large metal brackets with decaying rubber stops were mounted on the edge of the dock where large trucks would back up. Beer cans and empty cigarette packs littered the gravel and scraggly weeds that grew up from the base of the concrete foundation. The bay doors were closed. It was a faded yellow metal structure with a flat roof and looked like it hadn't been used in some time.

"It's noon on a Friday," Gus said. "You'd think they'd be open."

"Maybe this is an old address for the company and they just haven't updated their packing slips."

"The packing slip looked like it was from a desktop printer," Gus said. "Wouldn't be hard to update their address before printing it." His phone rang and he answered, listened, then hung up.

"Anything?"

"Yup. Or nope. Depends on how you wanna look at it," Gus said. "The address is the last known for McIntyre Machinery. They ceased operation two years ago, and when they were in business they manufactured tools."

"Tools?"

"Hammers, saws, screwdrivers," Gus said. "You know, tools."

"I've heard of them."

"But the company name on the packing slip, West Texas Tortilla Factory, doesn't exist," Gus said. "No business registered with that name, no tax records, nothing."

"The best Mexican food is always from the sketchiest looking places."

Gus shook his head.

I bent over and grabbed the handle to one of the three bay doors and pulled it up a few inches. "It's unlocked." With a grinding noise it gave way and rolled up into the ceiling of the building.

"We can't go in there," Gus said.

"You can't. I can." I stepped across the threshold into the building then turned back to Gus. "Help me. Help me. I'm in trouble," I said with no emotion.

"Well, damn," Gus said. "I hear sounds of distress from inside the building. Guess I gotta go in."

Gus followed me through the door and pulled the small flashlight from his belt, shining it around the large room. "Doesn't look like anything's been happening here for a long while."

We worked our way through the maze of industrial equipment, long dormant machines that once shaped and forged steel components. A thick layer of dust coated everything. I stopped and pointed, he aimed his light at the scuff marks in the dirt.

"Doesn't look like what you'd use to make tortillas," I said.

"I think we can safely assume at this point that there are no tortillas involved in any way."

"I'm holding out hope." I stopped and looked down at the cement floor. "Looks like plenty of foot traffic."

Gus cocked his head and looked around. "You hear that

humming sound?" He continued walking along the trail of footprints and I followed.

"It's getting louder," I said.

"Definitely electrical."

"Maybe it's the tortilla maker."

"Just stop it with the tortillas."

We moved slowly, listening as the vibration grew, stopping occasionally to reevaluate what direction it was coming from in the cavernous and echoing room. More foot marks were in the dirt on the floor as we approached the rear wall, then moved down along it.

In the back corner of the building we stopped at a pair of closed metal doors, the humming sound the loudest it had been. I reached for the doorknob as Gus instinctively pushed his suit jacket back and rested his right hand on the grip of his Sig Sauer P229 pistol. I turned the knob and pulled slowly, the hinges producing a long, slow groan. Bright white light spilled out into the darkness where we stood.

Rows of tables ran wall to wall from just inside the door, fifty feet to the back wall and the room was at least a hundred feet wide. Hanging from the ceiling were the sources of the humming sound, industrial lights emitting harsh white rays that spread out across the thousands of six-foot tall plants below them. The walls and ceiling were lined with shiny insulation to block infrared scans from law enforcement helicopters.

"Are those tortilla plants?" I said. "Do tortillas even grow on plants?"

"Please shut up," Gus said.

I walked into the large room.

"Watch your step," Gus said. "People who run marijuana crops don't tend to like strangers walking around."

"Especially feds."

The air was warm and humid. We walked from one end to the other looking down each long aisle until we reached the far wall. As we turned to work our way back, we both stopped. The muted sound of a siren could be heard from outside.

"Doesn't sound like the police," I said.

"Shit. It's the car alarm on my SUV," Gus said.

"Someone's trying to draw us out."

Back to the double doors to the grow room, I looked around the corner into the dark machine shop. The only light visible was from the single bay door we'd entered through. I motioned for Gus to move down the right wall, then go left toward the door while I went along the back wall.

Gus drew his weapon and began his slow egress, landing the soles of his dress shoes softly with each step. He scanned every angle while moving along the wall. I went left out of the grow room, then instead of staying along the back I bent over and zigzagged through the machinery, watching for the large power cables that stretched out across the dark floor. Halfway through the room in almost complete darkness, my shin struck solid on one of the big machines. I stopped and gritted my teeth to keep from screaming obscenities.

When I was one row over from the front wall, I stopped, took a knee, and waited. Moments later the dark shape of Gus moving along the wall became visible, his pistol still aimed down, his head on a swivel watching the room. I let him pass me while I stayed hidden and hoped he didn't see me and shoot.

I kept scanning to avoid missing movement in the darkness. Shades of black on top of each other plays tricks on your eyes and staring at one spot gives you tunnel vision. Finally I saw it, the shadows that didn't fit in, that moved among the static ones. Two shapes came out of the darkness and fell in behind Gus with no noise.

I stepped out and moved up behind the two figures as they closed in on Gus, my running shoes dulling any sounds my footfalls made on the cement floor. As the two shadows came within fifteen feet of Gus, I saw the quick glint of light reflect off shiny metal in the darkness. I closed the gap, then as I was almost on them, dragged my foot to make the slightest sound while going left into the row of machines again.

The two figures stopped and turned at the sound behind them. Gus spun around, his gun coming up as he did. I used the five-foot tall machine between myself and the figures, climbed up over the top in an effortless motion and came down from above them. As I jumped, my right foot landed on the shoulder of the nearest man, sending him toppling to the ground. The glimmer of the shiny pistol caught my eye as the momentum of my falling body brought me down onto the second person. I rotated as I struck the body, reaching out to grab the gun hand from both sides.

A gunshot echoed in the cavernous room and was followed by the sharp ricochets of the bullet off the cement and solid steel machinery. The body below me struggled to push me off as I brought my left elbow back into a jawbone that I couldn't see. With a cracking sound and a grunt, the body went limp under my weight.

I turned my attention back toward the first shape that was just beginning to climb back off the floor as Gus stepped in with his pistol aimed at the head, his flashlight blinding the man in the eyes.

"Hands on your head," Gus said.

"Thanks for the help," I said.

"Anytime."

CHAPTER 6

The two men sat on the cement against the loading dock wall, hands zip tied behind their backs. We'd searched and found a six-inch switchblade in one of the men's pockets along with several scratched off lottery cards, one of them a winner for $20. I shoved the lottery card into my pocket. The silver pistol was tucked in the waistband of my jeans. Gus came back from his SUV.

"One flat tire," Gus said. "Windshield is broken." He looked down at the detained men. "Who the hell are you and who runs this place?"

"Screw you," one of the men said, laughing as the other man looked down at his scuffed up work boots. "I think you broke my fucking jaw!"

"Perfect. Thanks for letting me know which one of you will talk," Gus said. "I'm going to take Mr. Personality with me to teach him how to be polite and not damage a federal agent's vehicle. You have a nice chat with his buddy."

Gus grabbed the man on the left by the back of his T-shirt collar and pulled him to a standing position. "That way. Now," he said. Once they were around the corner, I turned to the quieter of the two.

"You want me to list the charges we already have on you, or do you have a good idea already? My first guess, by your 1980's era Ocean Pacific T-shirt with holes and grease stains is that you're not the owner of this crop. My second guess is you'll have no problem telling me who's in charge to save your own ass from jail time."

The man looked up at me for the first time.

"Good. You understand me. Cause if your buddy talks first, he's the one who goes free. Now, what's your name?"

"Buck," the man said.

"Nope. Try again. What's your name?"

"It's Buck, I told ya."

"Nobody's name is Buck. Maybe back before you dropped out of junior high a few people started calling you Buck as a joke but you actually liked it and started telling people that was your name, but, no, it is not your real name."

The man lowered his head again and shook it. "Leslie," the man said. "Leslie Gaylord."

I nodded. "Damn. I'd go by Buck, also. Who owns this place?"

Leslie Gaylord looked back at the building. "I don't know who owns the buildin', I just know who hired me to work here."

"That's a start. Name?"

"Marcus Knowles." Leslie said it as if I should know the name, that it should instill fear in me, as if to imply "The Marcus Knowles."

I shrugged as if to imply I didn't give a shit. "Okay. And where would I find Marcus Knowles?"

"I only ever seen him here," Leslie said. "He drives a big Cadillac, a white one."

"Do you ever make deliveries for Mr. Knowles?"

"No sir. I'm jus' security," Leslie said. "I'm supposed to keep people from comin' in here."

"And you're doing a swell job with all the unlocked doors. If people do come in here, what are you supposed to do?"

"Make them leave," Leslie said. "Or if they won't leave, tie them up and call Mr. Knowles."

"There it is. Give me your phone."

"I don't got one," Leslie said. "Jerry has it."

"I'm guessing Jerry is the one my partner is having a chat with right now?"

Leslie nodded.

I walked to the end of the building, watching back to make sure Leslie didn't try to make a run for it. Even with hands tied behind his back, I wouldn't put it past him. Looking around the corner I saw the man I now knew to be Jerry lying face down in the dirt. Gus stood beside him staring at his own phone.

"Whatcha playing?" I said.

"Texas Hold'Em."

"Doing well?"

"I'm up 15k."

"Nice," I said. "Hey, you find a phone on him?"

Gus tossed me a flip phone he pulled from his jacket pocket.

"Thanks. And his name is Jerry if you haven't gotten that yet."

"Haven't really tried."

"Leslie up here is singing like a bird, so see if you can get anything out of this guy. He'll have a hard enough time in jail."

Jerry was trying to yell through his dislocated jaw as I walked away. "I'll tell ya whatever you wanna know!"

Back to Leslie I opened the phone and pulled up the recent calls and tapped the button to redial the last number. It rang three times. A man who sounded like he'd had a pack of cigarettes for breakfast answered, stretching each syllable out longer than it needed to be.

"Has it been taken care of?"

"Marcus Knowles?" There was silence for several seconds before the man spoke again.

Gus came around the corner with Jerry in tow and pushed him to the ground beside his co-worker.

"I guess it is not taken care of," Marcus Knowles said. The rasp in his voice made the soft vowels almost silent.

"Far from it. I'd like to have a talk with you. In person, preferably. That's if you want to keep your crop here intact. If not I can have the Texas Rangers, FBI, DEA, ATF, and everyone else on my speed dial here within the hour."

"No need," Marcus said. "I shall be there forthright."

"That's not what that means."

"Pardon me?" Marcus said.

"Nothing. Do I need to say come alone or is that implied?

Never mind, I'll just say it. Come alone."

I hung up and turned to Gus. "It's on."

He nodded. We moved Leslie and Jerry inside the building and reinforced their restraints, adding some to their ankles and connecting them together at the feet so there was no way they could run. Then Gus and I sat on the edge of the loading dock and waited.

"You have any plans this weekend?" I said.

Gus nodded. "Have a date tonight."

"Oh really. Who is it?" We were interrupted before he could answer.

The 1990's white Cadillac pulled to a stop and sat idling, the rumble of the exhaust from the American V8 engine audible from twenty yards away. The back right door opened slowly and a white Stetson cowboy hat barely appeared above the door frame.

Marcus Knowles stood five-foot-one without the hat and five-foot-eight with it. His dark blue fitted jeans appeared to be pressed with a razor sharp crease running down the fronts of both legs. The tri-color shirt contained large blocks of red, black and yellow and was as stiff as cardboard. The leather holster on his right hip looked brand new and held a Smith & Wesson Model 27 revolver, the barrel extending past the bottom of the holster to the man's right knee.

"What the hell?"

"I don't know," Gus said. "But it's kinda cute."

As Marcus Knowles walked toward us, he made a show of keeping his right hand out away from his revolver, as if ready to draw at any time.

"Thought I said come alone."

Marcus looked back at the Cadillac. "I do not myself drive," he said. "My chauffeur has been instructed to stay within the car."

I stifled a laugh as Gus spoke to cover the noise. "I have a call in to my office. If I don't respond in five minutes then every law enforcement office in Texas will be alerted and descend upon your little town."

"That shall not be necessary, Special Agent…"

"Ramirez," Gus said.

"Special Agent Ramirez," Marcus said. "I come as a businessman to make a business deal. I wish to have my men and my product unharmed. What is it you are seeking from this predicament? If you wished for the product, we would not be standing here right now, I do not believe."

"We're just looking for some answers." Gus turned to me.

"What can you tell me about this." I pulled the packing slip from my pocket and walked toward Marcus Knowles.

The man took a step back with his right leg and let his hand fall closer to the revolver.

"I'm not carrying." I held my arms up and turned around to show I didn't have a weapon. I continued walking toward the man. The silver revolver Jerry had been carrying was now locked inside Gus's SUV. I held the receipt out just shy of the smaller man's reach, making him step forward to take hold of it.

Marcus reviewed the document and handed it back. "I do not have any knowledge of this document," he said.

"Funny. It comes from a building you're doing business from. We're not here to bust you. You'd be face down with my size 11 running shoe pushing your mini Garth Brooks wannabe face in the dirt right now if we wanted to bust you."

Marcus Knowles grimaced. "It has become apparent that you do not realize who it is you are speaking to."

"Whom."

"Pardon me?" he said.

"It would be 'you do not realize whom it is you are speaking to.'"

"I do not appreciate being mocked," Marcus said.

"Then answer our questions and we'll all be on our way. Otherwise, it's getting pretty close to my partner's call-in time."

Marcus glanced behind me at Gus. "That is a packing slip for a shipment of product."

"Who's it for?"

"I do not reveal the names of—"

"Okay, we're done here." I turned to Gus. "Call in the cavalry."

"Gentlemen," Marcus said then paused. He looked us both over, giving himself a moment to decide what to do before realizing he had to talk or go to jail. "That particular client is one Benjamin Hubble."

"Like the space telescope?"

"The what?" Marcus said. "He is not in space. He is in the Army. That is all I know about the gentleman."

"How much product are you shipping to him?"

"More than one man would certainly be able handle," Marcus said. "What opportunities he makes with it is his business, not mine. I am a supplier, not a dealer."

I nodded. "Whatever helps you sleep at night. One last thing. I need an address to send the bill to."

"I beg your pardon?" Marcus said.

"The bill for fixing the windshield on my partner's brand new SUV. Either that or we'll charge you with destroying federal property."

CHAPTER 7

Buck and Jerry changed the tire on the SUV while we watched and they weren't happy about it. I could see Marcus Knowles' white Cadillac parked at the far end of the street. It left as we were about to drive off. The rear window was rolled halfway down and I saw the top of his cowboy hat barely above the glass.

I called Eva as we got back on the highway and gave her a few details about what had taken place. She had learned not to ask questions up front but knew that in my own time I would fill her in on anything she wanted or needed to know.

"You coming home?" she said.

"Not yet. We need to check something out. Hopefully later tonight."

We said goodbye and hung up.

"What are we supposed to be checking out?" Gus said. "I want to go home. I have a date tonight, remember?"

"We need to see about that name at Fort Hood."

"I already texted my office," Gus said. "I had them run a background on him. Benjamin Hubble is a Lieutenant Colonel. He's married with three kids and drives a red Corvette."

"Not really a good family car."

"No, and not really a car a Lietenant Colonel can afford, especially with a family," Gus said.

"You think he's dealing?"

"He's doing something with big shipments of weed."

"You get an address?"

"Of course I got an address."

"So we're going, right?"

He looked at his watch. "I need to be home by 6:30 to shower and change before picking her up."

"Deal." I made the motions to cross my heart.

Gus shook his head and pressed down on the gas pedal as he passed a semi.

"Oh come on, you love this." I had the stereo on and turned up with Guy Clark singing Dublin Blues. "Wanna tell me about her?"

Gus glanced at me. "Not really."

"Come on."

"Nope."

"Why not?"

"Just don't want to."

"You work with her?"

"God, no," Gus said. "That's the fastest way to never getting a promotion."

"So she doesn't work for the FBI," I said. "That narrows it down."

Two hours later, we pulled up across the street from Lieutenant Colonel Benjamin Hubble's home on the east side of Killeen, Texas. The red brick country rambler stood out in no way from the homes around it. On the right end of the house was a carport for two vehicles, the left space taken by a Chrysler minivan. On the right side was a vehicle with a light brown canvas cover over it, the Corvette logo embroidered on the visible end.

"Classy. I wonder if he has the black faux leather jacket with Corvette written down the sleeves, too," I said. "Man I always wanted one of those."

We sat in silence and stared at the house for a while. There would be the the occasional glimpse of movement as someone went past a window. Gus checked his watch every few minutes.

My phone vibrated. Shelley's name came up on screen.

"Who's that?" Gus said.

"My sister." I tapped the button to send it to voicemail. "I'll call her later. She's been talking about having Eva and me over for dinner. Probably trying to lock that down."

I searched online for anything I could about Hubble and Marcus Knowles but there was little to be found. Knowles probably didn't realize the internet existed and Hubble was too smart to let his private information end up out there. No social media, not even an account on LinkedIn. I thought about checking Tinder but decided I'd have a hard time explaining looking for men on Tinder to Eva.

"I'm hungry."

"Me too," Gus said.

"Shoulda grabbed something on the way."

"I'm gonna be starving tonight and pig out at the restaurant," he said.

"Where you taking her?"

He almost told me. "Nope."

"What, you think I'd show up there?"

"Yes, I do."

"You're probably right," I said. "I really don't respect personal space."

He sat up in the driver's seat and leaned forward.

"We have movement," Gus said.

A woman came out the carport door carrying a baby, two small children following her. The oldest child wore a soccer uniform. We watched as she struggled to get the baby in the car seat on the passenger side while arguing with the two bigger kids to get in the van and buckle up. Eventually everyone was strapped in and the minivan backed out of the driveway onto the road and sped away.

"No," Gus said.

"What?"

"We're not committing our second felony today," Gus said.

"Come on. The first one really doesn't count if it's an illegal drug operation."

"Even if it didn't, breaking into an Army colonel's home would definitely be frowned upon," Gus said.

"Okay. No B&E. We'll just look around outside." I pulled the handle to open my door. "No reasonable expectation of privacy. Someone gets home, we just say we're big Corvette fans."

"What size engine would that Corvette have?" Gus said.

"I don't know, an 80?"

"You just picked a random number. That's not even an engine size," Gus said.

"Okay. Someone comes, you talk. I'll just say I think it's pretty."

I pushed my door open. "What if he's home?"

"Three cars are registered to him and the wife, Cady Hubble, so one is unaccounted for."

We walked across the street to the carport and I ran my hand along the low top of the covered Corvette. "Of course he backs in. Because that makes total sense."

Behind the car I pulled the cover up to expose the trunk and tried to open it. With no luck I went to the driver's door, slid the cover up again, pulled the handle, and the door popped open.

"Who leaves the door of a $60,000 sports car unlocked in their carport?" I knelt down and looked inside the two-seater convertible. The tan leather still had a strong new car smell. I pushed the button to release the trunk for Gus. In the glove box I found the registration, owner's manual, and nothing else.

"You might wanna get back here," Gus said.

"Nothing boring ever happens when those words are said." I pulled myself out of the car and stepped back to the trunk and looked in. "It's empty."

"Smell it," Gus said.

I leaned over and sniffed the small black-carpeted trunk. "Marijuana." I pulled the edge of the stiff carpet back. Reaching down, I pulled the edge of the black carpet up and pulled out a green leaf. "Looks like some fell out."

"Want me to put a BOLO out on the other car?" Gus referred to the 'be on the look-out' request that can go out to all law enforcement to inform the issuer of a sighting but not to stop or detain the individual.

"I do, but I also don't want to throw any red flags. We don't know how connected this guy is. What about financials? Can you find out where he used his credit card recently without alerting everyone?"

"Of course I can," Gus said. "But this isn't a federal case. Hell, it's not even a case yet. I can't go using official channels on your witch hunt."

"You already requested the financials, didn't you."

"Yeah. Should have them by morning."

I looked at the door that went from the carport into the house, then turned my back to it quickly.

"Shit. Turn around," I said.

"What?"

"Turn away from the house. There's a security camera right over the back door."

"Goddammit, Eddie."

CHAPTER 8

I sat on the deck off the master bedroom in our bright red modern house just east of downtown. It was hers when we met, and still is technically, but she keeps telling me to call it 'our house.' I'd given up my apartment when I moved in and, although I was comfortable, it was still a mental adjustment.

Eva had dinner waiting when I got home. We ate in the kitchen, then she told me to relax while she cleaned up. I didn't know what I did to deserve this. I just knew I needed to do everything I could to keep from screwing it up.

I'd spent ten or so years in Virginia and D.C., a few months at other field offices here and there. The rest of my life was in Austin. The house I grew up in was still in use down the street from my old high school, my father's nursing home less than two miles from there. It wasn't a happy upbringing, being the son of a career Army man and not having any interest in joining myself. He saw the FBI as part of the problem, not the solution. He'd experienced firsthand, as Clem had, the mistakes on the part of so-called intelligence agencies on the hard working men and women of the military. Without a college degree, he capped out in career path and spent his last decade in the service pushing papers around.

Eva came through the door and handed me a tall glass with a lime wedge and salt along the rim. She sat down in the other chair with a glass of white wine. It was our favorite place in the house, close to bed for when we were ready to collapse at the end of a long day, and a view of downtown Austin above the other homes in the neighborhood. The television downstairs got little use. More often we'll listen to music in front of the fireplace than watch anything.

"Whatcha thinking about?" she said.

"I can't figure out what Clem's got himself into." I looked out at the lights of the buildings a couple miles west. "Can't imagine him doing anything illegal."

"Then he isn't," Eva said. "You know him far better than I do, probably better than anyone else. If you say he's in the white, he probably is. You just need to find out what he needs. He contacted you for a reason."

"You don't have to remind me of that." I glanced at my watch. "It's been nearly sixteen hours since the message and I'm no closer to finding him."

"Maybe he isn't looking to be found," she said.

I thought about that for a moment. "What do you mean?"

"Are you certain he wants you looking for him, or does he want you looking for something else? A man with Clem's training and background can disappear easily almost anywhere in the world. If he doesn't want to be found, he won't be. So maybe he just needs help with something that he can't handle."

"That's… kinda brilliant."

"Thanks." She smiled that incredible smile of hers. "I have faith in you," Eva said. "He does, too."

We sipped our drinks as Eva stretched her legs out and put her feet on my lap. This was one of the best things in my world. I put my hand on her and stroked the skin from her toes and up her legs to the bottom of the sun dress she was wearing. It was comfortable being with her, but never boring. We'd met under strange circumstances and I'd never wanted anyone but her since we met and I wanted her all the time.

"Did you buy any antiques today?"

"Nah," she said.

"But you had fun?"

"Oh yeah."

"Good," I said. "Sorry I had to bail on you."

"No apology necessary. I find it sexy that my man is so connected to his friends."

"You do?"

"I do."

We both have odd schedules, her as an emergency room doctor and me with the club and cases that keep me out long hours, day and night. But somewhere in there we find the time together, moments like this of casual quiet. Her skin beneath my fingers was calming to me.

When I left the FBI, it was to get away from the corruption of D.C. and the long hours. I was never lonely back then because I never had time to be alone long enough. I was always too concerned with opening up about my career with anyone. Some agents I knew would use their badge to get girls, and I was guilty of that a few times, but once I moved to the Joint Terrorism Task Force, security was too rigid. If pressed, I'd say I was an analyst with the FBI. Enough people had jobs in the D.C. area they couldn't talk about so that usually did the trick. There were women here and there, never anything serious for either of us, just fun and sex and no commitments. At least that part had changed. The stability Eva provided centered me. But with the bar and the cases, I don't make it to bed at a normal hour most nights, but then neither does she. So it works.

"What are you going to do next?" she said.

"In general or right now?"

"About Clem."

"Oh, right. That's a the million dollar question."

"I know you'll figure it out," she said. "You always do."

Drinks ran low and I went downstairs to refill them. When I came back through the bedroom, she was on the bed naked, one knee raised and a hand resting on her smooth belly. I took a sip of my margarita then sat the drinks down and pulled my T-shirt off.

CHAPTER 9

My phone vibrated and I grabbed it from the nightstand. It was a text message.

Gene Carroll

I didn't recognize the incoming number. I copied the message into a new text and sent it to Gus, then dialed his number.

Gus answered on the seventh ring. "What."

"Did you get my text?"

"It's 5:30 in the morning."

"Yeah, and did you get my message?"

"I did and I have no idea what it means," Gus said.

"It's from Clem. I think. I don't know who else would have sent it."

"Okay, okay. I'll check the name out and call you back."

Gus hung up before I could say anything else. I looked

over and Eva was still asleep. I always woke before her. Most mornings I got up for a run and a shower before she has her first morning wake-up yawn. Other days I stayed in bed beside her for hours just to be near her, to listen to her sleep, feel her warmth.

My phone rang and I answered fast to keep the buzzing sound from stirring Eva.

"Gene Carroll's name hit in San Antonio," Gus said.

"Excellent. You have his address?"

"I do, but he's not there."

"How do you know?"

"Because he's in the morgue."

"You could have started with that."

"I talked to the detective covering the case. He'll meet us at the scene. I'll pick you up at 8:00 to head down there."

After hanging up, I looked over at Eva and smiled as I always do when looking at her. As I stood to pull my jeans on, she rolled onto her back and looked at me.

"Is it about Clem?"

"Yeah."

"Find him."

"Okay."

"Do you have to leave right now?"

I glanced at the clock on her nightstand. "No. I have some time."

"Good. Then ravage me."

So I did.

Gus had us in the left lane, twenty over the speed limit.

"What about the sender?" I said.

"Did a lookup on your phone," Gus said. "The text came from a burner in San Marcos."

"A burner makes sense if he's hiding out."

Just over an hour later we pulled up in front of a small house on the east side of San Antonio. A tall, slender African American man stepped out of a Dodge Charger that was in the driveway. He was wearing grey slacks and a white dress shirt with the sleeves rolled up to the elbow and a holster on his hip.

"Who's this?"

"Detective with the local P.D.," Gus said. "It's his case. Agreed to let us in after I told him the murder may be tied to a federal investigation."

"Didn't know you had it in you, Gus."

"Who needs a long and distinguished career, anyway?"

The detective introduced himself as Herb Cuttler and walked with us to the front door. He produced the key and let us in. The living room was small with worn out furniture and a small flat screen television. The beige carpet had seen better days.

"What can you tell us, Herb?" I said.

"Call came in on Wednesday evening." The detective looked through the notes in his spiral bound notepad. "The girlfriend came home from visiting her mother and found him."

The detective showed us where Gene Carroll was found; his head part way into a closet in the one bedroom as if he was trying to hide. A single bullet had been put through his head from behind.

"Any drugs or weapons found?" Gus said.

Herb Cuttler shook his head. "No, sir. We more than expected it from a residence in this neighborhood, but the place was clean. Got some gangbangers around here, so we figure one or two of them came in here looking for money, something to sell, or just a hit to get through the night."

Gus and I stared down at the closet floor for a minute, each working scenarios through our heads.

"Any chance you could give us a few minutes in the house?" Gus said.

"Reckon I could, Special Agent Ramirez." The detective glanced at his watch. "Pleased to help the bureau. I have an appointment downtown in twenty minutes, so if you'll lock up, I'll leave you to it."

"Much appreciated."

As soon as the detective's car pulled away, Gus closed the front door and turned to me.

"This was no gangbanger," I said.

"That's for sure," Gus said. "You first."

"It's all wrong. Gangs are sloppy. They like a mess. It would have been AR-15s with rounds in all the walls," I said. "Definitely wouldn't have had him kneeling in the closet to off him."

"The next house is ten feet away," Gus continued. "That kind of firepower would have been heard and stray bullets would be in the neighbor's walls. Bangers aren't big on silencers." He stepped closer to the closet. "This was professional. Shot to the back of the head, likely suppressed. Gloves were worn so no prints. Mail is neatly stacked, drawers are closed. The shooter wasn't looking for valuables."

I went to the kitchen table and picked up an envelope. "A letter from the VA."

I pulled the paper out and read it.

"Statement of benefits received." I said. "Looks like Gene Carroll was in therapy."

"It's not much, but it's something."

We looked around the house more without finding anything useful.

Gus's phone rang on the drive back to Austin and he pressed the button to answer on hands free. "Ramirez."

The FBI agent on the other end of the phone spoke. "It's Jacobs. I got the info you wanted. Is now a good time?"

"I have Eddie here with me," Gus said. "What do you have?"

"Gene Carroll served in the Army from 2003 to 2007," Jacobs said. "He was posted to Fort Hood but shipped out to Forward Operating Base Fenty in Afghanistan in April of 2004. In March of 2006 he was sent back to Texas before his tour was up."

"Anything else?" Gus said.

"Not much. The address in San Antonio has been listed for him since 2007. Looks like he shared it with his girlfriend. His paychecks direct deposited into a joint account."

"Thanks," Gus said, then ended the call.

Gus glanced over at me, then back at the road. "Did Clem ever spend time at FOB Fenty?"

"He was a Ranger, so he went all over the place," I said. "But yeah. Fenty is part of Jalalabad Airfield. I know for a fact he at least flew in and out of there."

"So that's two with some form of tie to the same location, other than Fort Hood, of course," Gus said.

"What about Hubble?" I said. "We know if Hubble was in Afghanistan?"

"No, we don't." Gus dialed his phone again and asked Jacobs to do a deeper check on Lieutenant Colonel Hubble.

By the time Gus and I got to the satellite FBI office in Austin, Jacobs had the info we were looking for.

"Hubble was at Fenty from 2003 to 2008." Gus sat down behind his desk. "What's that mean for us?"

"It's no coincidence that every name involved so far was at the same base in Afghanistan at the same time." I walked behind Gus and looked out the window. "We need more data."

"But what data?"

"Everyone at FOB Fenty from 2003 to 2006, to start with."

"Not only would that be a huge set of data, it's probably impossible to get," Gus said.

"Okay. How about everyone from Texas at FOB Fenty during that time period."

Gus nodded. "The three names we have are all long term residents of the state. It would be a start at least, and bring the pool of names down to something manageable."

"How do we get it?"

"I know someone at D.O.D." Gus grabbed his phone and searched for his contact at the Department of Defense. "It'll take some time. You need to put in some face time in with Eva?"

"She's working. I'm all yours."

"I've noticed. Can't seem to get rid of you."

Gus picked up the desk phone and dialed. I listened as he caught up with the woman on the other end of the phone, to the point of flirting. The call turned more serious, bordering on begging when he explained what he needed then was silent while writing notes down. After hanging up, he leaned back in his chair.

"She'll do it," Gus said. "But she said it might not be exactly what we want."

"How's that?"

"There's no real logs of every service man and woman at a base at a specific time," Gus said. "Troops pretty much become numbers when they're on the ground. She said even when a squad goes out on a patrol, there isn't necessarily a list of names."

"Where does that leave us?"

"Flight manifests," Gus said. "She's pulling all inbound and outbound manifests from 2003 to 2006 for flights headed into and out of Fenty, and cross referencing with last known addresses to identify anyone who ended up in Texas."

"That should help," I said. "When will she have the data?"

"Tomorrow at the earliest."

I looked at my watch.

"Got a band at the club tonight. Wanna go hang out a while and have some beers?"

"I would but I have plans."

"Oh, really. Two nights in a row?"

Gus looked at me with his leave me alone expression, and I did.

CHAPTER 10

I walked through the door to Buddy's Music Parlor, paused, and looked around. The bartender was pulling several draft beers while the two waitresses worked their way around the room taking orders and delivering drinks.

The first band wasn't set to go on for another fifteen minutes and the volume of the crowd talking was louder than the pre-show music coming from the huge speakers.

I usually spent a lot of time here during the day working on bookings, catching up on paperwork, and double checking the numbers, though I trust my staff. I try to come for at least one night of shows a week when I'm not busy with a case.

The main act was from Dallas, but the opening band was local and played at least once a month, always drawing a good crowd from the college.

One of the waitresses saw me come in. I motioned for a beer, pointing toward my office in the back room where I found my desk empty. As always, paperwork was all put away and locked up in the drawers. The computer screen was dark.

Sherry brought the beer and went back to work the tables.

I thought about Clem and wondered where he could be. If he had indeed sent the text about Gene Carroll, he must be safe, but still in hiding.

I pulled my phone out and tapped a message to Eva.

How's your shift going?

A minute later a note came back.

Living the dream. A drunk driver hit a fire hydrant and ejected from the car, 38 stitches that he won't remember getting. Two college kids broke each other's noses fighting over a girl.

I read the message and grinned. Her weekend late shift stories were always entertaining. My phone buzzed again.

And a DOA, guy shot in the back of his head. Don't even know why they brought him in. I need a vacation. Will you take me on a vacation?

I stared at the last message then dialed Gus's number.

"You know I'm busy, right?"

"Then why did you answer?"

"I don't know."

"The E.R. just had a DOA," I said. "Guy shot in the back of the head, sounds same as Gene Carroll."

"Any more info than that?"

"No. Don't know anything else. Just got a text from Eva."

"Find out more then let me know," Gus said. "That's not enough to tie the two together."

I hung up and found the number for a police officer that helped me out occasionally and called him.

"This is Mendez."

"It's Holland."

"Whaddya want? I'm more than a little busy here."

"You working the shooting?"

"What do you know about it?" Mendez said.

"Not much, just that you have a head with a hole in it," I said. "I'm working something that had a similar M.O. down in San Antonio."

There were shuffling sounds and voices in the background, then Mendez came back.

"825 South Washington. Act professional." The phone went dead.

I took another sip of my beer. After dropping the glass at the bar, I was out the door and in my pickup headed west. Fifteen minutes later, I parked behind a row of Austin Police Department cruisers and unmarked cars with their blue lights on. I reached in the glovebox and grabbed an ID on a lanyard and pulled it around my neck.

As I approached the yard, an officer raised a hand to stop me. I held up my ID and he let me through. In the front door I looked around as Officer Mendez walked over and looked me up and down. I was still wearing cargo shorts, a Pantera T-shirt, and flip flops. Around my neck were my FBI credentials I pulled out for special occasions. The credentials weren't exactly official anymore, but I had an agreement with the bureau that allowed me to keep them as long as I was available to consult.

"I thought I said professional," Mendez said.

I pointed at the creds and Mendez shook his head.

"What happened here?"

Mendez turned and walked through the room and I followed.

"Call came in at 8:04 when a neighbor heard a single gunshot," Mendez said. "Two units responded and cleared the house. We found the deceased face down on the bedroom floor, one shot in the back of the head."

The house was clean and organized. There was a sofa, chair, and coffee table in the living room. At the end of the sofa was a lamp on a cardboard box. As we passed the kitchen I saw a blender on the counter with the cord wrapped up inside the pitcher. Mendez stopped and pointed into a room where two crime scene officers were pulling blood samples and prints. A queen sized bed was made, six decorative pillows at the head. I stepped in and looked down at the floor. A large dark red stain was on the brown carpet between the bed and the closet. In the closet were neatly hung clothes, several in dry cleaner bags.

"Who was he?" I said.

"Wallet on the kitchen counter has a driver's license that matched what we could find of his face." Mendez glanced at his notebook. "Jordan Hayes, 58."

"Know if he's Army or former Army?"

Mendez shook his head. "Haven't gotten a full background yet."

"Anything? Where he worked?"

"I'm no fancy private detective, but the van in the

driveway that says 'Hayes Plumbing, Established 1990' on the side gives me a hint."

I stepped to the kitchen door and looked out. The back half of an older Chevy panel van was sticking out of an oversized garage door.

"That's a large garage."

"It's for an RV. My in-laws have one like that up in College Station."

"Hmm."

"That all you have to say?"

"That's what I say when I'm thinking."

"Do you say it often?"

"Not really."

"So what do you think about this?"

"Doesn't line up with my case."

"Then I think you're done here," Mendez said.

I looked around once more, thanked Mendez, and left.

The night air rushed through the cab of the pickup and out through the sliding window behind me. Even though the temperature at 10:00 p.m. was still in the high 80's, the wind felt good. Sun June's album Years was on repeat, perfectly blending with the mood of the drive.

I was west of Austin on the two-lane Fitzhugh Road, going nowhere in particular. Eva was working. The bar was taking care of itself as it always did. Gus was probably sleeping or still out on a date. Headlights were far behind me as I approached the end of a straight stretch, turning the wheel to take the slight bend in the road, the lights disappearing behind the trees.

The text message was the last I'd heard from Clem and

I still couldn't be sure it had been from him. I kept hoping for another cryptic message to pop up, some sign that Clem was alive, but the screen stayed dark.

The image Officer Mendez described came to mind, a dead man with a bullet in his head, and the similarity to the body in San Antonio. The murder fit but at first glance, the victim didn't.

I passed Pedernales Falls State Park and kept driving. Eight miles later there were headlights again, closer than before. I slowed to roll through the small town of Johnson City. I made a right on 281 to head north to make a large loop past Lake Travis back into Austin.

After glancing at my watch, thoughts went to Eva, as they often do. It was almost midnight and she'd probably be taking her late night lunch break soon, but I'd never get to the hospital in time. She had a way of listening to me describe a case and simplifying it. Rarely did she give a suggestion—instead she'd boil it down to one question, one question that filled in a dozen missing pieces.

Eva was a cop's daughter, and though she had no interest in law enforcement, and even hesitated to ever date me because of the work I did, she understood it. I always felt that her career catered to it, listening to patients describe how they felt, what was wrong. She followed the clues to diagnose and treat.

I wondered what one question she'd ask me, what simple set of words would bring the light on inside my head.

I thought again of the house I'd been to tonight and the abrupt conversation with Mendez. There was something I knew I wasn't seeing, pieces that hadn't snapped together as they should.

Headlights suddenly hit the rearview mirror and I darted my head to the left to keep from being blinded. I was driving ten under the speed limit and the vehicle behind me pulled to the left lane to pass.

The front of the car came in to view, an old Chevy Malibu station wagon with peeling window tinting showing hints of the boxes and piles of newspapers and trash inside the vehicle. Then behind the car was an old orange box trailer, with only the "U-Ha" left of the original paint job. The new owner had likely bought it from an auction after it had been put out of rental service.

I stared at the trailer as it slowly pulled farther ahead, the lights of my truck fading on it with the distance. The scratched and worn drawing of a man with a shovel over his shoulder and large pan for gold prospecting was on the back of the trailer. SKAGWAY, AK was written under the drawing. I wondered if the trailer had ever actually been to Alaska or had spent its life in the heat of the southwest, taunting drivers on the road with thoughts of cold air, freezing water, and striking it rich with a gold nugget the size of your fist.

The last bit of his headlights on the orange trailer as it pulled farther away highlighted the remainder of the words "We Sell Boxes."

I read the words three times, smiling. It was the middle of the night, but I wanted to go to the office and dig into the data. Gus wouldn't be there until 8:00 in the morning though. I relaxed back into the drive and enjoyed the night air.

CHAPTER 11

Gus walked into his office and I was sitting there with two cups of coffee, mine almost empty already.

"One of those for me or are you double fisting?" Gus said.

"I could certainly use them both." I handed Gus one of the tall cups.

"You're up early."

"Late, actually. Haven't been to bed."

"Why so eager?" Gus sat down behind his desk and tapped his keyboard to wake his computer and log in. "Wait a second, how'd you get in here?"

"Piggy backed one of your agents."

Gus shook his head. "Dammit. They know they're not—"

"I went to that crime scene last night," I interrupted, too excited to wait and too sleep deprived to care about being rude. "But the guy wasn't Army. He's been a plumber since the early '90s so I asked one of your agents to do a check on him. No military service."

"So it was a waste of time," Gus said.

"Nope." I turned a stack of papers in front of him, a finger pointing to a yellow highlighted line with the name "William Jennings" and an address.

"What's this?" Gus said.

"That's the house I was at last night."

"But you said he wasn't Army?"

"Yes, I did. Jordan Hayes was killed in that house and was not in the Army. But William Jennings lived there before him, and served two tours. His last at Forward Operating Base Fenty."

Gus stared at the paper and read the address and the accompanying information, his head slowly shaking until it stopped. He looked up at me.

"They hit the wrong house." Gus said.

"Right house, wrong month," I said. "Last night's victim moved in three weeks ago. A month before that, William Jennings moved out."

"So last night was connected, they just made the wrong guy dead."

"Yes, but there's something bigger than that going on here," I said. "Whoever's behind this is using the same data we are. We have the same outdated address information for William Jennings."

Gus reached for his phone and dialed.

"Who are you calling?"

"D.O.D." He put the call on speaker.

"Sheila Baxter." The woman's voice was soft and a little bit sexy.

"Sheila, it's Gus again."

"Well, hello. Twice in one week?"

"Yeah. You're on speakerphone with me and my colleague Eddie Holland," Gus said.

"Ooh, a three-way?"

Gus shook his head. "We have some questions about the data you sent."

"All business today, I see. What do you need?"

"Is there any way to tell if anyone else has accessed this specific data set?" Gus said.

"No. I did a custom query of the database using the criteria we discussed," Sheila said. "But, if you give me specific names I can see if anyone has requested their DD-214's."

"What's that now?" I said.

"Every service member has a file, their DD-214. They can request the full file at any time. But anyone can request a shorter version of the DD-214 of any service member. They get logged in the system as having requested it."

I looked at Gus and he nodded.

"Sheila, this is Eddie. Can you check William Jennings to see if anyone has checked his file?"

Clicking sounds came through the speakerphone.

"I have three William Jennings, but only one in Texas," she said. "And it does look like his info was requested about three months ago."

"Can you tell me who requested it?" Gus said.

"Now, now, Gus," she said. "Remember what we talked about a few days ago?"

He put his face in his hands and I could tell he regretted being on speakerphone now.

"I sure do, Sheila," he said.

"When are you gonna make that happen?" she said.

"Soon."

"How soon?"

He wouldn't make eye contact with me. "In a few weeks. I need to clear some things before I can leave town."

"I'm holding you to that."

"I promise," he said. "Now who requested the info?"

"Name listed is Benjamin Hubble," she said.

Gus and I sat up straight in our chairs.

"You're certain about that?" Gus said.

"You questioning my work?"

"No. Can you cross reference for any other records Benjamin Hubble requested?"

Some clicks, pauses, and clicks again.

"I have about a dozen names, all requested by him on the same date," she said.

"Send them to me?"

"They'll be in your inbox in seconds, dear," she said. "Call me next week to make plans?"

"I will."

He hung up. I stared at him.

"First of all," I said. "What did you two talk about the other day that requires you to leave town?"

"Dinner."

"Dinner? You promised to take her to dinner?"

"She was doing us a favor," Gus said.

"She lives in D.C.!"

"Virginia, actually."

"And where are you taking her to dinner?"

"Inn at Little Washington."

"So, a $400 flight then at least a $700 dinner."

"Shut up," Gus said. "I should make Clem pay for it."

"What about your new girlfriend? This is getting very exciting."

A pinging sound came from his computer and he checked email.

"Got the list of names and addresses," he said. "Here's Jennings. Only address is the same house where the plumber got killed."

"We'll find him." I said. "Right now, whoever killed Jordan Hayes last night thinks Jennings is dead, so he should be safe for now."

Gus turned and started tapping on his computer and making phone calls. I tapped out a message on my phone. Ten minutes later, Gus was swearing loudly.

"Every record has the same address for him," Gus said. "He lived there for nearly ten years."

My phone pinged. I glanced at it. "Got him."

"What?" Gus said.

"I found Jennings' current address."

"What the the hell?" Gus looked at his computer and back at me.

I turned my phone screen to him. "Asked Shelley. She called the electric company using her law firm's name to get a forwarding address for Jennings' final bill."

"Well, shit." He logged off his computer. "Let's go."

The address looked like an apartment on the other

side of the city and Gus drove. As we got close, we were between two strip malls, then stopped in front of a package store.

Gus looked at the address. "It's a private mailbox."

"Damn."

"What now?"

"See if he got any mail?"

"We don't have the key."

"Give me a minute."

I went into the store and found the box. A few letters were visible through the tiny window. A woman came in the front door with a paper coffee cup.

"Oh, I forgot to lock up while I ran next door," she said.

"Not a problem," I said. "Looks like I forgot the key to my mailbox anyway. I'll have to come back later."

"Oh phooey on that." She set her coffee down and went behind the wall of mailboxes. "What number is it?"

"210," I said. "Jennings."

"Right. I knew that, just couldn't put the name to the face."

I'd never seen the woman before but went with it.

"Happens to the best of us."

She came back around the wall and handed me the small stack of mail.

"Thank you, dear. I appreciate it," I said.

Back in the SUV I flipped through the letters.

"Did you just steal mail?"

"No. She handed it to me," I said. "We have an electric bill, a bank statement, and a flyer for an RV shop."

"That was worth a federal offense."

I looked out the window. "Did you check what cars Jennings has?"

"No."

"At the house last night there was a garage for an RV, and he got mail from an RV shop."

Gus begins to nod with me. "So he has an RV."

He made a call as he drove us back to his office.

"No RV but he has a Ford F-250 pickup and a registered fifth-wheel trailer," Gus said. "I have a BOLO on it."

CHAPTER 12

Waiting is the worst part of any case. You feel useless and used at the same time. I left Gus and went home. I was still tired from the all-nighter, but didn't feel like sleeping. It was a lot easier in my twenties than it is in my late thirties. A long hot shower refreshed and relaxed me. Wrapped in only a towel around my waist, I sat down on the balcony outside the bedroom and air dried. I wanted a margarita, but settled for a beer. It wasn't the time to get tipsy or drunk.

I thought about getting dressed and heading to the bar. There was always paperwork to do, orders to place, though Vic, my manager and bartender, handled it most of the time. The bar wasn't always my plan. Gus and I bought it when Buddy, the original owner, died on the floor in front of the stage, shot by an assassin trying to kill me. I'd gone to high school with Buddy and it seems obvious to say I felt responsible, so I bought the bar. His family had no interest in it and sold it to me for way below value. The story of what had happened pulled more business in at first and I was able to book some slightly bigger acts and the place supports itself now, allowing me to pay Vic and only go in when I needed to. I never looked at it as a way to get rich as much as a way to be part of my city. Gus was a mostly silent partner. He was in for a little less than I was as a financial investment, leaving me to make all the day-to-day decisions.

My left foot was up on the railing and my head leaned back, eyes closed. I heard a sound and instinctively reached for my cellphone on the table then realized it was the sliding glass door behind me, Eva getting home from work.

"Whoa, letting it all hang out there?"

"Sometimes a nice air dry is good for the boys."

"Nope." She shook her head then turned and walked inside. A minute later I heard the shower start up.

I looked down at my towel. "What do you say, boys?"

Assuming they'd agree with my plan if they could speak, I got up and went into the bathroom, dropped my towel on the floor and stepped into the shower with Eva.

After the shower we ended up in bed, naked and wet and giggling. We made love then I curled up around her. I leaned in for a kiss and was met with a huge yawn and knew it was time to let her sleep.

Dried and dressed, it was still only 11 a.m., so I made eggs and toast and checked my phone every few minutes for a message. Finally it vibrated and I read the message.

Got a hit on the truck in Oklahoma. Meet me at TXDOT at AUS in 30 min.

That was incredibly fast for a BOLO, especially from another state. I grabbed my Glock from the floor safe in the pantry, threw a loose fitting button down on over my Sunny Sweeney T-shirt to cover the pistol, put on my straw porkpie, and left.

In the time since returning to Austin, I'd stopped questioning how Gus does what he does. While I was off pushing papers in D.C. with occasional trips overseas to track terrorists, he was moving from field office to field office making connections that mattered. Sure, I could give you details on the big players in the Middle East, but he can get you planes, guns, and backup about anywhere in the world. He's had two fishy looking guys in a Jaguar hand me a Glock in Ireland, a Texas State Police plane fly us to Padre Island to follow a lead, and once arranged a safe house in Istanbul for a witness with a single phone call. Now we're airborne on the way to Oklahoma to chase down an RV in an aircraft that usually transports senators and representatives to Washington D.C. and back.

The Beechcraft King Air 200 twin engine plane landed at the small Tahlequah Municipal Airport with plenty of runway to spare. I'd reclined in my seat and napped for two hours while Gus tracked Jennings' location through Oklahoma State Patrol on his phone. While waiting for the BOLO, he'd had Jennings cellphone tracked and that hit immediately, allowing him to focus the lookout. The call came less than ten minutes after that.

"He stopped at an RV park on the Illinois River last night and hasn't moved since," Gus said.

The plane came to a stop in front of a hanger. The pilot came out of the cockpit and popped the door open.

"You'll wait for us?" Gus said.

"Yes, sir," the pilot said. "We have three other aircraft on the ground in Austin in case anyone from the capital needs a ride."

An unmarked silver Oklahoma State Police Chevy Tahoe was parked beside the hanger. Though it had no official markings on it, no one would confuse it for a privately owned vehicle. It had ram bars on the front, steel wheels, and a spotlight mounted beside the window. We climbed down from the plane and greeted the trooper.

"How long will it take to get there?" Gus said.

The trooper glanced at his watch. "Should take about 20 minutes. We'll do it in less."

Highway 10 outside Tahlequah is a collection of twists and turns along the Illinois River. The large SUV body rolled with each curve taken at double the marked speeds and twelve minutes later we rolled into the riverside RV park that catered to locals and tourists wanting to canoe the slow moving river.

An unmarked car was parked at the entrance, and the troopers raised fingers in half waves to each other. The cruiser pulled in front to lead us to Jennings' RV. When the car slowed, the trooper's hand came out his window and pointed at a Ford pickup with a long fifth wheel trailer attached and kept rolling to go up the next row and block the vehicle from the front. Our SUV stopped behind the trailer.

"Water and electric is still hooked up and the trailer has the leveling jacks out, so they aren't running," the trooper said.

Gus and I got out of the SUV and approached the trailer. Our driver moved off to our right and I saw the other trooper covering the far side. A window shade moved.

"They know we're here," Gus said.

I knocked on the metal door and spoke loudly. "William Jennings. Please come out unarmed, hands where we can see them. We just need to talk to you."

The doorknob clicked and the door swung open. A man stepped down to the ground.

"William Jennings?" I said.

"Yeah. Who are you?"

"I'm Eddie Holland and this is Special Agent Gus Ramirez with the FBI."

"What do you need?"

"Answers."

CHAPTER 13

The travel trailer was larger inside than I thought it would be. Gus sat across from Jennings at the kitchen table and I leaned on the counter between them and the door. Jennings' wife was outside with the troopers. Coffee had been made and we all sipped from white mugs.

"Why are you running?" Gus said.

"I'm not running," Jennings said. "I'm retired. Traveling the country with my wife. Livin' the American dream and all, you know."

"Looks like you're running," I said.

Jennings shrugged. "You say tomato, I say screw you."

"I'm going to say some names," Gus said. "You tell us if they mean anything to you. Gene Carroll."

"Yeah." His head was hanging down now, staring at the floor.

"How?" I said.

"Served together overseas."

"At Fenty?" Gus said.

"Yeah."

"Okay. That wasn't hard. How about Clem Akins."

Jennings shook his head. "No."

"You sure?"

"Wait, black guy, tough as rocks?"

"That would be him."

"Met him once, maybe. He didn't speak much."

"Sounds about right," I said. "Benjamin Hubble"

The man was quiet and still. His breath changed as if he were trying to control it.

"Nah."

"You sure about that?" Gus said.

Jennings stayed quiet.

"You know Gene Carroll is dead?" I said. "He was shot in the head on his bedroom floor."

"And two nights ago a man was killed in your former home on Washington Avenue, gunshot to the back of the head," Gus said. "Because they thought it was you. But instead it was a fifty-eight year old plumber who had the misfortune of renting your old house."

Jennings looked up, his face red. "I knew about Gene. Read about it in the paper and a couple guys called to tell me. Didn't know about the plumber."

"So, let's try again. Benjamin Hubble," Gus said.

"It's not safe," Jennings said. "I just can't." He glanced out the window at his wife talking with the troopers. The sound of her laughter filtered in through the thin walls of the trailer.

"Two men are dead, that we know of. More are at risk. A friend of mine is missing," I said. "We just need information and you can disappear to the middle of nowhere for as long as you like."

"What's the connection, William?" Gus said. "Why Gene? Why the attempt on you? What does Hubble have to do with it?"

"Hubble's nothing." Jennings sat up straight, a blast of courage or anger or fear pushing him. "He was just the messenger. But if you crossed him, then you were fucked."

Gus glanced over at me before continuing.

Gus said, "Who did Hubble work for?"

"Ortiz. We all worked for Ortiz, okay?" Jennings said. "Goddamn the two of you. If it gets back that I talked, I'm dead, my wife's dead."

"Ortiz have a first name?" I said.

"Leo. Leo Ortiz."

"Okay. We're getting somewhere now. Ortiz was in the Army also, over at Fenty?" Gus said.

"As far as I know, yeah. We all worked for Ortiz, but Hubble made the connections, found the talent, delivered the orders. He was a smooth talker, worse than an Amway salesman."

"What's this Ortiz look like?" I said.

"I don't know. We only ever dealt with Hubble."

"You never saw him?" Gus said.

"Not once."

"And what did you do for Hubble and Ortiz?" I said.

Jennings leaned back and looked out the trailer window at his wife again. I could tell he was about to step over the line he'd drawn for himself in self preservation and he was scared, but that he also wanted to do it, to get it out there. The man exhaled loudly.

"We stole fuel from the Army," he said.

"Fuel?" Gus said.

"I've heard about this," I said. "A few went to jail over it from a different base."

"Yeah. It wasn't an original idea, but it was a good one," Jennings said. "Ortiz ran it all. Drivers who ran the fuel routes were approached. If you weren't into it on your own, they found something on you and blackmailed you into it."

"Which was it for you?"

Another look out the window. His head shook slowly back and forth. "I couldn't take the chance of her finding out. It would have ruined her. Would have ruined us." He paused to collect himself. "There was a party on the base. Someone, Ortiz I'm guessing, had some local, how can I say… talent… brought in, along with cases of whiskey. I got drunk and—" His wife laughed loudly outside. William Jennings almost went over the edge, fingers gripped the table as his body tensed in the way you do when trying to hold back your emotions. "There's pictures. Of me and a woman."

We let his thoughts hang for a moment.

"I thought it was over when I got out," he said. "But Hubble walked up to me in a Walmart parking a couple months ago. He didn't bluntly threaten me, but it was sure implied."

"What did you do?"

"I told my wife enough for her to understand why we

were leaving everything behind. Left a lot out. She knows I was wrapped up in something bad but she doesn't know about the women. Not gonna lie, it was rough for a while."

We sat in silence except for the voices coming from outside.

"We met in high school. I was two years older," he said. "We dated but I was eighteen and she was sixteen so most we did was hold hands. The second she graduated I asked her to marry me."

"Were most people forced into it, would you say?" I said.

He nodded. "One or two younger guys, fools who thought they were owed something in life, they went willingly. They bragged about the money they were making while the rest of us kept quiet and found ways to hide the cash from our families until we could find an excuse for it."

"How'd you you hide the money?" I said.

"Shipped it home to my brother in Denver. He hung onto it, no questions asked," he said. "My wife never knew I had it until Hubble showed up again and I told her."

"What did you do with it?" Gus said.

William motioned his arms around him. "You're sitting in it. I deposited a few thousand at a time over a couple years then paid cash for the trailer and the pickup."

Gus and I looked at each other. He nodded and left the trailer.

"William, I'm not investigating this crime," I said. "I'm trying to find my friend. But if in the course of our search other law enforcement finds out, they may come looking for everyone involved."

William Jennings nodded.

"I won't be giving them your name or anything you told us. I'm not saying I agree with what you did, but I'm not going to be the one to take you in."

"I appreciate that," he said.

"Maybe make sure you have enough put away somewhere for your wife," I said. "Somewhere it can't be found. Just in case."

"I will."

We were back on the Beechcraft and flying out of Tahlequah after a stop for food. The trooper recommended a place called Katfish Kitchen. We took it to go and spread the family style meal out on the table on the airplane. Two six-packs of beer washed the food down easily.

"We have a dozen names," I said. "Some we know. Clem, Jennings, Gene Carroll. The rest we don't."

"It would be good to know if they're alive or have been threatened," Gus said. "Only a couple are still in the Austin area. The rest are all over the place. We'll check the locals and I'll put some calls in to field offices to follow up with the others."

CHAPTER 14

We sat in Gus's SUV outside an apartment complex not far from my old one. We sipped cherry limeades from Sonic and watched the door of the building. Gus had chosen the music and had Jason Isbell's album Something More Than Free playing and I wasn't complaining.

"Bo Murphy. He works for the school district, maintaining buses." Gus glanced at the time. "7:45. He should be heading to work soon."

After the known names on the list, there were only two left in Austin. The rest were spread out across the country. Gus had made calls to field offices and where possible agents were checking them out. One call had already come back from Little Rock that the person's home was empty, boxes and clothes thrown about as if they'd left in a hurry.

It was thirty more minutes before Bo Murphy came out

the front door of the apartment building and got into a green two-year-old Ford Mustang we knew was registered in his name and paid off. We fell in behind him, not worried about being spotted.

We followed him across town, waited on the street while he went through a McDonald's drive-through, then into the parking lot of the bus maintenance facility. Gus stopped the SUV behind the Mustang, blocking it in. I got out and walked around the Explorer and stood next to Gus.

The man sat in his car, looking at us in the rear view mirrors then rolled his window down and yelled back to us.

"What do you want?"

"To talk," Gus said.

"You police?"

"FBI." Gus held his badge up.

Bo Murphy climbed out of the Mustang and looked around while walking over to us. He held a large soda cup with the red, white, and yellow striped straw and sipped from it. I wanted to think he was sipping guiltily, but wasn't sure what that would actually look like.

He was in his late 30's and not too tall. The years since the Army had taken a toll on his lifestyle; his work shirt fit snugly around the beginnings of a beer belly. He wiped his wet hand from the condensation of the cup onto his work pants.

"Okay. Talk," Bo said. "I need to get to work. Got bills to pay."

"Like the payments on that Mustang?" I said.

He shrugged.

"You know Gene Carroll?" Gus said.

"I knew him, yeah."

"Then you know he's dead."

"Heard some gangbangers got him."

"That's one story," I said. "You don't seem too torn up."

"Didn't lose sleep over it."

"How about William Jennings?" Gus said.

"Heard something happened to him, too." His responses all verged on sarcasm.

"You did?"

"Home invasion or something like that," Bo said.

"Right." I looked over at Gus who gave the slightest nod.

"Benjamin Hubble," I said.

"What about him?"

"You worked for him."

"Don't know what you're talking about," Bo said. "Knew him, wouldn't say I worked for him."

"What would you call stealing fuel from the Army and selling it to the highest bidder?"

He shrugged again. He was good at it, very natural. I made a mental note to practice shrugging. "Never heard nothing about it."

"If you're not going to be upfront with us then get out of here," Gus said. "Go to work."

"What, you not arresting me?"

"Nah," I said. "If we wanted to arrest you, we'd have been through your front door at 6:01 this morning with FBI SWAT flattening you to your worn shag carpeting stained with Bud Light and Domino's pizza."

He squirmed enough to tell me he finally understood we were in control.

"Has Hubble been in touch with you in the last two months," I said, "or at all since leaving the Army?"

"No."

"You lying to us?"

Another perfect shrug. "No."

"We're done here," I said.

Bo walked away, then stared back at us as he entered the building.

"He's sweet," Gus said.

"The epitome of southern charm," I said.

Gus crossed the two lanes of traffic to get back onto the road. "Guess he's still working for Hubble."

"Seems that way," I said. "Which means Hubble will know that two feds are asking around about him."

Gus glanced over at me. "Well. A fed and a beach bum."

"I prefer South Texas Chic."

"Mmm hmm."

"Got one more from the list that lives local, right?" I said.

"Yeah. Hector Santos," Gus said. "I have a car on him now. Hoping to hear back from some other field offices soon about the ones out of the area."

"Maybe less likely they're still working for Hubble and Ortiz remotely. Not really a telework kind of job."

"True, but still good to know if they're alive or dead."

The stereo buzzed with a cellphone call and Gus glanced at the caller ID.

"It's Phillips, he's the one following Santos." He tapped the button to answer on speaker.

"You should probably get over here, boss," Phillips said.

"What is it?"

"Three police cars just came in hot. Now an ambulance is pulling up."

"On our way. Let me know if anything else happens."

Gus hung up and turned left on a red light, two cars screeched to a stop to keep from hitting us. We were across town in less than ten minutes and stopped behind the police cruisers. Officers were walking around and talking while a few were up on the porch of the small house.

Phillips walked up to our window. "Santos is holding a gun under his chin. Doors are locked. His eight-year-old son called the cops but is too scared to open the door now."

"They have contact with him?" I said.

"An officer on the porch is talking to the boy through the door. A cell on speakerphone in the house gets to Santos."

We were out of the SUV and moved through the crowd of police until we found the officer talking to Santos on the phone. Gus flashed his badge, the officer muted the phone.

"What the hell does FBI have to do with this?" He looked over at me in my cargo shorts and ten-year-old Tontons T-shirt. "You sure you're FBI?"

"It's casual day at the office," I said.

"I didn't get the memo about casual day," Gus said. "We're working a case and were on our way to talk to Mr. Santos."

"I can't just put you on with him," the officer said. "This is a hostage situation."

"Has Santos said his son can't leave?" I said.

"No, but he's locked inside the house."

"Have you asked Santos to tell his son to leave?"

"No. Not yet. We've only had contact for five minutes."

"Should have been your first request."

The officer looked at Gus and shook his head. He raised the phone to his ear.

"Hector, you still there?"

A voice came through the phone. "Yeah. Don't know where I woulda gone to."

"Good. Hector, why don't you tell your son to leave? We have officers waiting outside the door. They'll take care of him."

"I don't know," Hector said.

"Do you want him to see this, Hector? Is this something you want him to experience?"

The phone went silent. In the commotion of idling police cruisers and officers walking around, we couldn't hear if there was still an open connection. Then we heard Hector Santos talking to his son.

"I want you to go out there, Julian. Unlock the door and go. They'll take care of you."

With no protest, the door opened and the boy walked out. His pants were wet in front and he was crying. A female plainclothes officer took him by the hand to a police van.

"That's good, Hector. Thank you. We'll keep him safe."

I patted Gus's jacket and felt his notebook. I pulled it out of the breast pocket. After scribbling a note, I handed it to the officer. After reading it, he looked at us. Gus nodded.

"Hector. I have two men here from the FBI. They know about Fenty and want to get you to safety."

CHAPTER 15

I stood on the front porch, an Austin Police Department bulletproof vest on over my T-shirt, my Glock hidden between my back and the vest.

"You sure you wanna do this?" Gus said.

"I am. A guy in a suit or a uniform probably isn't the best first impression."

"Neither is a guy who looks like he sleeps on a park bench."

"Touché."

With my hand on the doorknob I called out. "Hector, it's Eddie. I'm coming in."

The house was clean and everything in its place. Hardwood and mid-century modern furniture blended into a seamless floor plan.

"I'm in the house, Hector."

"Right here."

Startled, I turned to my right. Hector was sitting on the first landing of the stairwell, his back to the wall.

"No line of sight from windows here," he said. "Didn't want a sharpshooter taking me out before I could do it myself."

"Makes sense," I said. "I never understood that, aiming guns at someone trying to kill himself."

"Right?" he said.

I stepped to the left so I could see his gun. It was big. A .45 probably. Wouldn't leave much for his son to see.

"So what's going on, Hector? You're really scaring your boy."

"He isn't mine. Came home from Afghanistan after an eighteen-month deployment and had a six-week-old infant at home."

"That math doesn't add up," I said.

"Still love him, though. People always say he looks like me," Hector said. "The real funny part is his real dad is white."

"You wanna put the gun down so we can talk? I'll stay over here. Not going to try anything." I leaned against the far wall. The front door was still open and I could see Gus looking around the door frame.

Hector hesitated, but eventually the gun lowered, the barrel now faced the wall but where it could easily be raised back to his chin or at me.

"Why you trying to off yourself?"

"Damn. They teach you that at negotiator school?"

"I'm no negotiator. I'm just a detective."

"Thought you said you were FBI?"

"I am. Or was. For a long time. Got to be too much so I took a break and haven't gone back. I still work with them a bit, but on my own terms."

"Sounds like a good gig."

"Ups and downs."

"Guess this is a down."

"Nah. Sitting in my car for thirty-six-hours trying to get photos of someone playing tennis when they're supposed to be injured from a car crash is the down part."

He gave a grin but it didn't have any feeling in it. "Still sounds like a good gig. Maybe I shoulda become a private detective after the Army. Would be more fun than being an insurance adjuster."

"Looks like insurance does well for you," I said.

"It's fine. My wife is an aesthetician. Makes good money."

"I'll nod and pretend to know what that is."

He grinned again, a little more heart this time. For the first time I started to believe I could talk him out of this and hadn't made a huge mistake coming in here.

"You said you know about Fenty," he said.

"I do. A little. Piecing it all together."

"You trying to catch them?"

"Hubble and Ortiz?" I said. "Not how this all started out, but my buddy outside the door is real FBI and they're definitely interested in them."

"Gene's dead," he said.

"Yes. But Jennings isn't."

"Really? I'm glad. He's a good man."

"Seems to be."

"You protecting Jennings?"

"No. He's taking care of himself and his wife. I think they'll be okay."

Hector nodded. "Hubble was waiting by my car after work one night. Didn't say a word at first, just waited for me to unlock the doors and got in with me. We drove around for an hour."

"What did he want?"

"To make me work for him again."

"Not interested, I'm guessing?" I pointed at the .45.

"You could say that."

"What's he have on you?"

I saw motion to my right outside the door as the SWAT van was unloading. As subtly as I could I motioned no to Gus.

"Girls? Drugs?"

"Nothing that fun. I enlisted at sixteen with forged documents."

"What now? How'd you even do that?"

"My mom and older brother died in a car crash. Dad was a drunk and totally lost it. Wasn't sober again for a year. I had to identify the bodies. There wasn't much left. I don't know why, but right there in the morgue, staring at him, I gave them my name instead of my brother's. Nobody questioned it. There was no investigation. Just another dead Latino in San Antonio. So a month later I took his birth certificate and went to the recruitment office."

"Damn. That worked?"

"It did. The newspapers even said it was me in the crash."

"And if you got caught—"

"Would have been kicked out of the Army, probably put in jail for fraud. Would lose all my benefits, retirement, VA access. I planned on being a lifer. Only bounced out to get away from Hubble. I got a wife and three kids. Sorta."

"What about the money you made from Hubble?"

"Donated a bunch of it to my church anonymously. Used a bit to pay off bills."

"Are you for real?" I said. "You're the most morally upstanding criminal I've ever met. And I've met a lot."

"Thanks?"

"So, about that gun."

He looked at the pistol. "Thought if I died my wife would get my benefits and I'd be out from under Hubble and Ortiz."

"They probably wouldn't pay out over a suicide."

"Started thinking about that after all the cops showed up. By then it was too late to just yell 'my bad.'"

"Where's your wife and kids now?"

"Wife's at work," he said. "Daughter is working at Sonic down the street and my son is probably at football practice."

"Let's get you out of here, somewhere safe. Away from Hubble until this thing is over."

"I'd like that."

His thumb hit the release on the left side of the gun and the magazine dropped out, then with a quick pull back of the slide, the remaining round ejected from the barrel and clinked to the floor.

CHAPTER 16

It was 6:30 in the morning and we sat in my pickup a few doors down from Hubble's house. We wanted to follow him to work, see if he made any stops along the way, then repeat on the way home in the evening. Gus brought breakfast and we'd grab something out for lunch and maybe drive through the military compound to see where the Lieutenant's car might be.

The morning went about as expected. Hubble came out of the house and took his early model Honda Pilot, leaving the Corvette under its cover on the carport. He drove the most direct route to Fort Hood and disappeared through the gate.

After driving around the large base with no sign of the Honda, we left through the gate Hubble had entered and parked where we could watch for him to exit and waited. It was 6:20 when the SUV came out and we fell in a few cars behind it. My king cab F-150 blended in since it was Texas. I wondered how we'd fare it we were in San Francisco. Or Vermont. We followed for fifteen minutes. Hubble stopped at a grocery store. By the time he came out, the sunlight cast longer shadows.

Hubble didn't head toward his house and we stayed as close as we could without risking being spotted.

"I don't like it," Gus said.

"What don't you like?"

"Doesn't feel like he's going anywhere, just driving. There's more direct routes to everywhere we're going."

"Maybe he's just delaying going home," I said. "Or waiting for a call to make a drug deal."

"Perhaps," Gus said. "I just wanna be on the record that something stinks."

It was ten more minutes before Hubble made a right turn into an abandoned Walmart parking lot, the new one having been built three blocks down the road. The large shell of a building sat with no signage and the few windows in front whited out with paper and small signs for the leasing company, no other businesses eager to take on an 80,000 square foot space that would always look like a Walmart. It's like an Asian restaurant that buys an old Pizza Hut with the red brick and pointed roof. You might order the Pad Thai but you'll always smell the burned pepperonis.

"This has drug deal written all over it," I said.

The Honda went down the right edge of the lot then made the left behind the building, an access area maybe fifteen feet wide for delivery trucks to go through.

"No way to keep from being spotted," Gus said.

"All or nothing, baby."

"Don't call me baby," Gus said.

"Sure thing, sweet cakes."

I waited a few moments before turning left behind the building. The Honda was nowhere to be seen. We rolled slow, watching the back of the building on the left and the tall graffiti covered fence on the right.

"Where did he go?" I said.

No sooner had I spoken than a beaten up Crown Victoria pulled out in front of us from a loading dock. Three guys in hoodies carrying bats and crowbars jumped out.

"Shit. Told you it stank," Gus said.

I threw the shifter in reverse and hit the gas before looking in the mirror. The truck took off quickly from the big V8. After thirty feet, we struck solid on something and threw us around the cabin.

"What the hell." I looked out the now shattered back window. A trash dumpster had been rolled out behind us while we were distracted by the thugs in front of us. Two more men were behind the truck now.

"Five guys," I said. "A couple look like they may be carrying underneath their shirts, but they're probably only supposed to scare us."

"I think they're doing a bang up job at it. Kudos to them." Gus checked the chamber on his Sig and put the weapon back in its holster. "I'm not really wanting to shoot anyone tonight."

"There's an axe handle behind the seat," I said. "You take that."

"What are you going to use?"

"The bat that the guy on the left is holding."

We were both out of the truck and moved to flanking positions to not get surrounded by them. The two guys that were behind the truck moved up but didn't engage. Three on two, for now. Those are odds I'll take any day, especially with Gus beside me.

I moved to the outside of the man on the left. His dirty red hoodie had a faded logo on the front that I couldn't make out. His feet moved a lot, too much, almost hopping around and I knew right away he was far more scared than I was.

He swung the aluminum bat at me but was sloppy about it. His arms extended too far, his shoulders rolled over, all pushing his balance forward. Logic would say to let him continue the motion forward, grab the bat, throw him down. But I hate logic. I much prefer to counter momentum. I stepped in to get another swing out of him and it worked. He committed as I took a quick step back and felt the air off of the bat as it went past me, then rushed in while I knew he was just a bit off balance from reaching out.

My left arm extended and came around into a hook, my fist struck him in the temple while he still had forward motion. He was unconscious before his body even started to fall. His arms drooped, no brain online to control them, and I casually took the bat out of his hand as his limp body collapsed to the ground.

Two on two.

A glance at Gus and he had the upper hand even with two guys working him. The axe handle was held with two hands as a shield, stopping the strikes from an aluminum bat and a crowbar. The handle wouldn't hold up much longer to the metal striking it.

The crowbar came at him overhead in an attempt to reach past the axe handle and strike his head. Gus had the handle held up to block but the moment the impact should have happened, he spun out to his left, the handle swinging out away from his body in a circular path toward his attacker in some West Side Story meets ballroom dancing type of move he'd likely made up on the spot. The heavy metal tool created sparks when it hit the concrete and the axe handle created a hollow thud when it struck the back of the man's head.

Two on one.

The remaining man in the fight held his wooden baseball bat in his right hand, extended down to his side. His grip told me he knew what he was doing with it. The sunlight was all but gone and we were halfway between two streetlights from the road on the other side of the tall wooden fence, so all movements were becoming obscured in competing shadows. A feint to the right sent shadows going four directions.

I looked back and the other two men were still outside the fight radius. Neither looked ready to engage, leaning on my broken truck.

Gus moved right, I went left, putting our final opponent between us. He looked back and forth at us casually, the bat not moving at all. He was waiting us out, wanting an attack to defend against and give a counterstrike. That wasn't something I wanted to see.

"Who sent you?" I said.

A grin.

"Hubble?"

The slightest shrug.

"Ortiz?"

There was something, it was small, but a hesitation, perhaps shoulders tensed a bit.

"Yeah. It was Ortiz."

"You don't know a damn thing," the man said. He took a fast step toward Gus, causing him to back up, then the bat was coming for my head faster than I thought was possible. I cut the distance by rushing in to at least get hit by the smaller part of the bat.

The strike came just above my forehead as my back spun with the centrifugal force of his swing, stepping inside his radius to match his motion, my left elbow extended out, making hard contact with his jaw at the same moment the bat glanced off me. I felt skin tear, the instant coolness of exposed blood.

Gus was behind him. The axe handle struck three quick blows to the man's kidneys. As he folded forward in pain, the handle came around his neck and was pulled up, a loud gurgling of spit mixing with air trying to figure out if it needed to go out or come in. I stepped in with a side kick to his abdomen as Gus let go and the man fell to his hands and knees. His arms gave out and he sprawled onto the ground.

"Good moves," I said.

"You too," Gus said.

Gus leaned over to check the man for a wallet. I watched his body to make sure he wasn't ready to move and attack again.

The sound came from my right, soft, muted, a scuff on the ground, then my body was swung around from the impact on my abdomen.

My eyes searched into the faded darkness of the building, the silhouette of a slight man, one of the two who had waited behind the truck. They hadn't looked like fighters. I took them for visual backup, not heavies to engage in battle. I was wrong. I moved and on my second step was swung around again just as Gus yelled to watch out. In the flash as I rotated I saw Gus, his Sig now drawn and moving, trying to track a target.

My legs gave and my knees struck the cement, but the lowered height gave Gus an advantage. I heard the light footfall to my left, the prelude to another hit. It was followed by the loud crack of the 9 millimeter round exiting the barrel, echoing off of the cement block wall of the store. A grunt, a stagger in the darkness, then four feet running. As they passed under the light a hundred feet away, they were only thin, dark blurs.

CHAPTER 17

My body shook as I opened my eyes and squinted at the brightness of the morning sun. I barely remembered getting home, much less making it up the stairs. Every part of me hurt and I tried not to move.

We'd been stuck behind that building another two hours as police came to take the three men away that we'd subdued. The other two were in the wind. A medic looked in my eyes with a flashlight and put a bandage on my forehead where the bat had broken skin. There were the typical warnings I was used to: if I got dizzy or vomited, get to the emergency room in case of a concussion.

I tried to roll off my side and stopped, willing a huge bottle of ibuprofen to appear in front of me. It didn't. But Eva did. She came through the door with a sigh.

"Finally," Eva said. "Get out of bed. I've been trying to

wake you up for hours."

"What's going on?" I moved slowly and felt the pain in my back. "You okay?" She put her hands on my shoulders and helped me to the edge of the bed.

"I'm fine but you're bleeding all over the sheets."

I turned and looked at the cream colored sheets. A streak of blood ran where I'd been laying and was smeared into the bed.

"Oh, shit." I stood up quicker than I should have, my head swam, and I pulled at the top sheet to take it off the bed.

"Forget that right now." She helped me into the bathroom and turned me around. "Let me get a good look."

"What's back there? Did I get shot?" I quickly ran through the fight in my head and didn't remember any guns but couldn't say for certain. I did get hit on the head pretty hard, so I could have forgotten.

Eva dropped her head and closed her eyes for a moment. "What did I do to deserve this?"

"What?"

"There are just too many questions. How could you not know if you've been shot? And why would you even have been shot? Didn't you feel any pain? It looks like you've been bleeding for hours."

"It was a strange night," I said. "Things got a bit out of hand."

"Drinking too much and losing your car in a game of strip poker is a bit out of hand. Coming home with what looks like knife wounds on your back is quite a lot more than a bit out of hand."

"Can you fix it? We have any Band Aids?"

"Fix it? It's a pair of half-inch deep gashes four inches long," she said. "You need stitches. I don't even know how you're standing up right now. From the looks of the bed, you need blood, too."

After she put a pair of butterfly bandages over each cut, she threw a pair of my shorts and a tee shirt at me. "Get dressed. We're going to the E.R."

"Why didn't the paramedics find this last night?" I said.

"The cuts are incredibly clean," she said. "Something very sharp went through there, and probably very fast. Your skin held together while you were standing up so there may have been minimal bleeding until you were lying down. Your black T-shirt also hid any blood that came out, which probably stuck the cotton shirt to your skin, creating a bandage, of sorts."

She lined her car seat with towels and I got in, a large bottle of water thrust in my face.

"Drink. A lot," she said.

The car jerked to a stop when she saw my pickup parked on the street. The tailgate was smashed into a V and the rear window was gone.

Her head turned to me with an expression I'd never seen before and I couldn't put an emotion to it. It was somewhere between astonishment and extremely pissed off.

She drove with no concern for potholes and speed bumps, either not realizing that each one sent a spike of pain through me or completely knowing that and doing it on purpose. I hoped it was the former but knew it was the latter. Her form of payback.

My phone rang and I fished it out of my pocket, a groan from the pain caused by the stretch. A text from Shelley.

Call me. I need to talk to you.

I typed a quick message back.

Got hurt last night. On the way to the E.R. Will call you later.

The emergency room was quiet and Eva had called ahead. A nurse took me back immediately and after a check of my blood pressure and the wound, an I.V. was run into the back of my hand with fluids and blood. A series of injections around the two cuts numbed me and once I felt no pain I fell asleep.

Gus was sitting beside the bed when I woke up. The light green curtain was pulled closed around us and I heard voices and activity in another part of the emergency room.

"Why do you look so… healthy?" I said.

"Because I didn't get stabbed twice."

"Valid."

I tried to sit up and felt the pull of the stitches on my sides and slowed down. Gus took my hand and helped me get vertical. The I.V. was gone, replaced with a large Pokémon Band Aid across the back of my hand. Eva's touch, I'm sure. A plastic pitcher of water was on the metal table. I poured a cup and drank it all.

Gus leaned back and forth, looking at me.

"What are you doing?"

"Waiting to see if the water is going to spray out your sides," he said.

"Nice. I think I remember everything from last night. We won, right?"

I worked my way around the bed to see if my legs still worked. Everything seemed solid enough, but I wouldn't choose to run a marathon right then.

"Sure. We won. Like it was some street fight between the Greasers and the Socs."

"Yeah. Screw those Socs." I looked over at him. "Wait. Which would we be?"

"Good question. I mean, as law enforcement we'd be 'the man' so would that make us Socs?" Gus said.

"I really hope not. Though I would like to have a madras shirt and a Mustang."

My shorts and T-shirt were in a clear plastic bag hanging off the end of the bed. I could see the blood on the shirt. "Damn, my favorite Spoon shirt."

"Don't you have like six of those?"

"Yeah, but this one's from the Soft Effects show in 1997. It's irreplaceable."

"First world problems," Gus said. "You busting outta here?"

I wanted to, but the short walk around the bed proved to me I wasn't ready.

"Nah. Eva would kill me. I think I'll sit a while and drink more water."

"Probably a wise move."

"Anything on the three guys from last night?" I said.

"Two were your average street thugs, no military, long rap sheet," Gus said. "The third was at Fenty same time as Hubble."

"That the last guy? He looked ex-military."

"Yup. That one," Gus said. "He's on our list, so at least we don't have to go looking for him. An attorney tried to bounce him on bail but he had some outstanding tickets and a past assault charge so he's sitting in lockup. The other two are gone."

"Was it Hubble that sent the attorney? The guy didn't look like he kept one on retainer."

"Can't prove it, but a good bet he was behind it," Gus said. "I don't think the other two guys have any knowledge of Hubble and Ortiz's past military dealings. They're just hired locals."

"Disposable," I said. "I think next time we'll go directly to Hubble instead of trying to follow him."

"I'm game for that," Gus said. "So far neither of our cars are handling this case very well."

I exhaled and pulled the curtain aside to see what was happening in the Emergency Room. One person was being treated a few beds down, otherwise it was quiet. "We're not any closer to figuring out where Clem is or what he needs."

"We may not have an address, but I think we're doing exactly what he wanted," Gus said.

I turned to Gus. "William Jennings was blackmailed into working with Hubble and Ortiz."

"Right."

"And he said most of them were."

"You don't think Clem was part of it, do you?"

My history with Clem was short compared to with Gus. But I felt I knew him well. We'd talked a bit about life before the FBI for me, but couldn't think of one conversation about him before the Army.

"I don't but it's worth looking into," I said. "Can you pull his record?"

"You sure you want to go there?"

"If something shitty comes out of it but he ends up alive and never talking to me again, it'll be worth it. If he gets hurt or worse because we didn't dig, I wouldn't be able to handle that."

"I'll get it going," Gus said. "How long you gonna be out of commission?"

"Not long. I have to get back out there."

"We'll make sure not to get into any more fights," Gus said.

"Can you really promise that?"

"Hanging with you? No." He looked at the time on his phone. "I need to get to the office. I'll call you when I have any info on Clem."

He pulled the curtain aside then looked back at me. "Stay gold, Ponyboy."

CHAPTER 18

Eva drove me home. I rested while she put together lunch for us, mostly leftovers from the last few nights. We sat at the counter and ate while she let me ramble through my thoughts on the case. I'm sure I was at times incoherent in my comments, moving from one topic to another as I tried to put pieces together. I couldn't imagine how much worse it would have been if I'd taken the Percocet she left on the counter for me. Last time I took some of those I ended up having a long conversation about chemtrails with a homeless guy on 6th Street.

She changed the bandages on my two knife wounds, checking the stitches as she did. The local was wearing off and the pain came in strong. I swallowed three acetaminophen and chased them with beer. Still better than Percocet.

"You have to take it easy," she said.

"I will."

The way she looked at me told me she didn't believe me. I didn't believe me either. Truth was that as soon as I could, I would be back out trying to figure out where Clem was.

I told her about the fuel theft ring in Afghanistan. American soldiers used fake ID's and forged requisition forms to fill tanker trucks full of gas and diesel as if they were delivering it to the military bases, but would actually already have it sold on the black market in Kabul or Jalalabad.

Ortiz had been the mastermind of the Fenty ring, but so far was a ghost with no record in the files received from the D.O.D. Jennings had never met Ortiz and Gene Carroll was too dead to ask. Clem was our next to question, once we could find him.

The doorbell rang and Eva went to answer. She came back with Gus behind her.

"Thought I'd check on the patient in person," Gus said. I rarely saw him dressed casually anymore. His dark grey and black suits were how I expected to see him. He was now wearing blue jeans and a light yellow button down shirt with the tails out.

"He's relaxing more than I thought he would," Eva said. "But I have to go to work later and I know he's going to fly the coop as soon as he can."

"Awww," I said. "You know me so well."

Gus shook his head. "Figured. That's why I drove over to talk instead of calling or texting. Didn't want to give him an excuse to come find me."

"That's appreciated," she said.

"You bring new information," I said. "Come, sit before me and speak."

Gus looked at Eva. "He talking like that because of the blood loss?"

"No. He's talking like that because he's an idiot."

Eva sat beside me and Gus took the chair to my right.

"Got something back on Clem," he said. "It's not much, but about all I can get."

"What is it?"

"We know his military record well enough. That man has received about every commendation a noncommissioned officer can get."

"You'd never know it," I said. "He keeps everything locked up. Never seen him in dress blues to see his medals."

"He's as humble as they come, that's for sure," Gus said. "Before the Army, there isn't much. Born and raised in Oak Cliff. A few school records available show less than average grades."

"Oak Cliff woulda been rough back then," Eva said. "My parents still live in Dallas and Oak Cliff is almost completely gentrified now, but when I was a kid it was still not a great area."

"Exactly," Gus said. "Which makes the final part more interesting."

"What is it?" I said.

"He has a sealed record from the juvenile courts when he was seventeen."

"Oh, really," I said. "And when did he enlist?"

"About a month later and still before his eighteenth birthday."

"So he had a parent sign off on him going into he Army," I said. "Sounds to me like the judge gave him an Army or jail offer."

"Definitely," Gus said. "What he did, we don't know, but there's a chance Ortiz found out and tried to use it against him to help with their illegal operations."

"When we find him we can ask him," I said.

"There is the other possibility," Gus said.

"What's that?"

"That he did work with them."

"I just don't see that," I said.

"I don't either, but he does have a sealed record, so he did something bad enough to risk jail time."

"You have a point, but he was already a Ranger by the time he got to Afghanistan," I said. "I can't see him risking everything."

"Even if he was being blackmailed?" Gus said. "We don't know what's in that record. Could have been shoplifting at the mall."

"Clem doesn't strike me as someone who hung out at the mall as a teen."

The points were valid, though I didn't want to believe it. But the evidence toward it was strong. There was the apparent attack on him at his house, then him going on the run. That along with other men from Hubble's merry band of pillagers already having been killed didn't make him look good. But the Clem Akins I knew was a career Army man, a devoted soldier. He wasn't wrapped up in patriotic bravado, just in serving and doing the best damn job he could do.

Gus was invited to stay for dinner but made his excuses

and left. Which then brought up the question of what to actually have for dinner. We'd scavenged the remaining leftovers for lunch and stomachs were starting to rumble.

Then my sweet, lovely, beautiful Eva said the most amazing thing.

"We could go out for tacos."

I folded myself as gently as I could to get back into her Fiat 500, the lure of tacos acting as an anesthetic. Though I'd suggested a restaurant closer, she opted for the casualness of the Capital Taco food truck, and before long we were sitting at a red picnic table on South Lamar inhaling our meal.

We had finished and were getting back into Eva's car when I saw a familiar vehicle pull up on the other end of the lot where the food trucks park. Gus got out of the driver's door of the green Nissan sedan, his personal vehicle that didn't see much use. I was about to yell to him when the passenger door opened and a woman with long red hair got out.

"Is that Gus on a date?" Eva said.

I smiled. "Yeah. It is."

"You want to go talk to him?"

I watched as the redhead took his hand and they smiled while walking to the taco truck.

"Nah," I said. "Let's leave them alone."

CHAPTER 19

It was just after midnight when my phone rang on the nightstand. I was out of bed, into the hallway, and headed down the stairs as I answered it.

"What's up?"

"Hubble made several purchases tonight," Gus said. "Looks like he filled the tank on a car, but not until after he spent just over a grand at REI and another few hundred at an Army surplus store just off campus."

"So he's either going on the run or going camping."

"Looks that way," Gus said. "But there's more."

"Always lead with the more. The more is always better."

"I got an alert on Clem's card," Gus said. "Looks like he only has one credit card. At 11:14 p.m. there was a single charge for $1.79."

"What? Where was it? And please don't say Mexico."

"Balmorhea, Texas," Gus said.

"Where the hell is that?"

"About six hours due west of Austin," Gus said. "Population of less than 500 people."

I tapped to turn on the speakerphone as I searched for Balmorhea on the maps app, moving the image around.

"Shit."

"What?" Gus said.

"Davis Mountains State Park. It's the map on his office wall." I stared out the sliding glass door under the deck to the small back yard. "He's trying to get off the grid."

"Then why'd he spend two dollars at a gas station?" Gus said.

"So we'd know where to find him. He drove six hours without using a card for gas. He wanted to send a signal to me and knew we'd be watching his cards."

"Why Davis Mountains?" Gus said.

"Clem is an Army Ranger. He could disappear in that park and never be found."

"You really don't think he's just camping?" Gus said.

"He wouldn't go completely radio silent except for one tiny charge on his card after calling me for help if he was just camping. He wants me to find him. Or find something."

"Eddie, you're the only person I know who failed your camping badge in boy scouts."

"True. But you passed yours. How soon can you pick me up?"

"Thirty minutes."

I snuck back into the bedroom and tried to quietly

slide the louvered closet doors open to get my cargo pants out when the plastic wheel at the top of the door let out a screeching sound against the metal runner.

"What are you doing?" Eva said.

"Sorry. I was trying not to wake you."

"You leaving?"

"We have a lead on Clem. I might be gone a couple of days and may not have cell reception."

"Sounds like a story to go meet up with some slutty chick," Eva mumbled.

"Baby, you're the only slutty chick for me." I bent over the bed and kissed her forehead as she groaned then went back to sleep.

After dressing, I went to the pantry in the kitchen and moved a basket full of different teas from the floor. I raised a wooden panel that hid the small safe with a digital lock, tapped in the numbers of the combination, and took out my Glock 17 in its tactical nylon holster along with two extra loaded magazines and a box of ammunition.

The floor safe was a compromise. Even as a cop's daughter, Eva didn't like firearms loose in the house, but she knew they were a necessity in my world. I'd spent most of my adult life with a loaded gun within reach of my pillow so having it locked up on a different level of the house took some getting used to. She agreed to a top-of-the-line home alarm system and a baseball bat under the bed. I figured I could beat my way to the gun if we were invaded.

I disarmed the alarm and set the timer to rearm once I was outside, then pulled the back door closed behind me and turned the knob to make sure it was locked.

Gus pulled up as I got to the curb. I threw the duffel bag I'd quickly packed in the backseat of the Explorer beside the two backpacks we took from Clem's bunker. He was out of the SUV and walking to the other side.

"You're taking first shift."

I pulled the seatbelt on and looked over at him. He had his head resting on a pillow with the seat fully reclined.

"You brought a pillow?"

"Shut up or I won't let you use it while I'm driving."

We headed west out of the city on US-290. I wanted coffee but knew I'd need to get some sleep once Gus was awake and ready to drive. The highway was empty and the big SUV rolled easily. The large screen had the GPS up and mapped to the gas station where Clem's card had been used. Painfully, I left the stereo off to let Gus rest.

Once on I-10, I opened the engine up and set the cruise control. The new SUV had me reconsidering my old and now battered F-150. It was quiet enough to hear myself think and the heated seats felt really good. I still miss my Karmann Ghia I had before the pickup but could get used to something so effortless to drive.

It was another hour before Gus sat up.

"Find me coffee and I'll drive," he said.

A few miles later I exited into a truck stop in Segovia. Gus got a large coffee and I grabbed a case of bottled water. Back on the road Gus drove while I tried to sleep after finishing a whole bottle, still needing fluids. I reclined and closed my eyes.

The flatness of the land as you go west in Texas is intoxicating. Straight stretches of road lull you into a dream only to be snapped out of it when the highway makes the slightest curve to the left or right, surely the brainchild of a road engineer to keep people alert. The scarcity of headlights coming at you is so numbing that when a car eventually comes from the other direction you feel compelled to stare out the window to see who else is on the road in the middle of nowhere in the darkest hours of the night.

I slid forward, the seatbelt stopping me from going to the floorboard, when Gus came to a stop at the one gas station in Balmorhea, Texas. The sun was coming up from behind us casting, a red glow across the building.

"We're here?"

"Wherever the hell 'here' is," Gus said. "Sadly I feel this may be the last dregs of civilization we'll see for a while."

We walked into the gas station where a teenage boy was leaning over the counter on his elbows, his face staring at the cracked screen of a cellphone.

"Excuse me," I said.

"Wha?" the boy responded without looking up.

"Excuse me."

"Which pump?" The boy still hadn't looked up.

I looked at the name tag on the wrinkled shirt and spoke firmly. "Ernie."

"What?" He finally looked up.

"Were you working last night at 11:15?"

"Nah." Ernie turned his attention back to the phone.

"Please don't make me take that away from you. I just have a few questions."

"Shit, man," Ernie said. "Just tryin' to text my girl."

"We'll only take a minute. Who was working at 11:15 last night?"

"Ernie," Ernie said.

"You're kidding me, right?"

"Nah," Ernie said. "That's my dad, Ernie Sr."

"Of course it is. Where is Ernie Sr. right now?"

"At work," Ernie said.

"But he works here."

"Yeah."

I turned to Gus. "Even Abbott and Costello would've slapped this kid." I looked back at Ernie. "So if your dad works here and he's at work right now, where is he?"

"In the back room," Ernie said.

"For the love of—" I turned to the door to the backroom.

"Uhh, you can't go back there. Employees only," Ernie called after me.

"Just call me Ernie and it'll be okay." I went through the swinging metal door and the boy went back to his cellphone with a shrug.

The back room ran the width of the building and was lined with racks of sodas and beer. A wire cage full of cases of cigarettes and chewing tobacco sat with the door propped open by a pony keg of Bud Light. At the far end of the room I saw Ernie Sr. sitting at a desk made out of shipping pallets and walked up behind him. An old laptop computer was open on the makeshift desk and a video of two naked women having sex on a cheap leather sofa was playing with the sound turned down low.

"How's the movie?"

"Shit!" The man jumped up so fast he knocked the top

of the desk off the legs and it all began to fall to the right. "Goddammit all to hell." Ernie Sr. caught the edge and pulled it back to desk form. He slowly let go in case it tried to fall again.

"Sorry. Didn't mean to scare you." I didn't sound too convincing.

Ernie Sr. finally turned to look at me. "Who the hell are you?"

"I could tell you but in the end it doesn't really matter since I'll be leaving soon and you'll go back to watching what appears to be very bad porn on a laptop running Windows 95 and in ten minutes you won't even remember I was here."

"Huh?"

"Ahh, now I see the family resemblance. You were working last night at 11:15, right?"

"Uhh, yeah, I… who are you?"

"Again, doesn't matter. 11:15 last night a man came in. It was dark out. Probably not many people coming in that you don't know. Maybe driving an old army Jeep. Ring a bell?"

"Well, I don't… wait a second, there was that one nig—" he looked up at me and paused. "There was a black guy, real tall, looked strong but had a limp. Wasn't driving a Jeep, though."

"That could be him. What else do you remember? What kind of car was it?"

"Was a Chevy sedan, I think. Silver. He paid cash for the gas but then used a credit card to pay for a cup of coffee. Really pissed me off," Ernie Sr. said.

"Why'd that piss you off?"

"He had plenty of cash but used a card for the coffee. We gotta pay for every credit card that gets used," he said.

"You care how much the station pays in credit card fees?"

"I own the station."

"Oh, really. Good for you. I'll be sure to keep you in mind on Small Business Saturday."

"Huh?"

"Nevermind. Did the man say anything about where he was going?"

"Nuthin' I can remember," he said. "Except he asked somethin' funny."

"What was it?"

"He asked if there was any buffalo around here."

"Buffalo?"

"Yeah. Buffalo," he said.

"What did you tell him?"

"No."

CHAPTER 20

"Buffalo?" Gus said.

"Yeah. Buffalo." I popped four acetaminophen in my mouth and took a drink from a plastic water bottle.

"That's weird."

"Ernie Sr. thought so, too."

Gus sat in the passenger seat with his phone in hand and moving the map on the screen with his finger. "Hmm."

"Hmm what?"

He handed me the phone. Centered on the screen in the maps application was a highlighted point in the mountains to our west called Buffalo Trail Scout Ranch.

"A Boy Scout camp?"

"Yup," Gus said.

"You think that's where he is?"

"What else around here has buffalo in the name?"

"He asked about buffalo on the chance that we talked to Ernie Sr. and he told us."

"At this point? Sounds like something he'd do."

"Worth a shot." I pointed the SUV south down TX-17 and worked our way up the mountain into the state park. The drive only took half an hour and we pulled into the small settlement of buildings.

Pale teenage boys in jeans and T-shirts, wearing hats with wide, floppy brims to block the sun, were walking around carrying buckets to the ruins of an old house. I parked at the edge of the camp and we walked up toward the buildings when a tall, thin man came out of the nearest hut and stepped in front of us.

"Help you?"

"We're looking for a friend of ours."

"This is a private camp," the man said. "We take our boys' safety and privacy very seriously, so whoever you're looking for probably isn't here."

"Can we just have a look around?" Gus said.

"No, sir. Can't have that." The man glanced back at the scouts carrying out their projects. "The parents count on us to keep strangers away."

"I understand," Gus said. "Thanks for your time."

Gus turned and headed to the truck and I took a double step to catch up. "What are you doing? Let's just drop the badge on him."

"This isn't official business." Gus climbed in the passenger door and pointed to the other seat until I relented and got in.

"You obviously didn't see what I saw," Gus said.

"A bunch of boys being forced to do manual labor?"

"No. Well, yes. But at the far end of the camp, just past the last building on the right."

I strained my eyes through the dirty windshield. "Okay. What am I looking for?"

"Just keep looking until you see it," Gus said.

I scanned left and right until something caught my eye. I cocked my head at the shape and color of the vehicle sticking out from behind the farthest building. "Looks like a silver Chevy sedan."

"Finally," Gus said.

"It isn't much to go on. It's a pretty common color."

"But it's here, and we're here."

"True. So if he is here, how do we find him if they won't let us look around?" I said.

"You ready for some hiking?" Gus said.

"Not really. I was stabbed twice."

"If they won't let us up close, we go further away," Gus said.

"Is this some kind of riddle? I hate riddles."

"Inside the two backpacks we took from Clem's house are high-powered binoculars," Gus said. "We'll drive back a couple of miles, then park and hike up that ridge on the east until we can get a full view of the camp."

I looked at the mountain. "Climb that?"

"What did you do in your Boy Scout troop?"

"The guy who ran it was a locksmith. He taught us how to pick the locks on all the doors at the Presbyterian Church where we had our meetings."

"At least it was something that you've used in your career," Gus said.

"Damn straight." I put the truck in reverse, backed into an open area, then drove away from the camp. Two miles down hill I parked on the side of the road. We went through the backpacks and took out anything we didn't need and replaced them with bottles of water.

"Take some of those out of yours and put them in my pack," Gus said. "Don't need you splitting your stitches three miles into the hike."

I didn't argue. The hike was going to be hard enough with two knife wounds that I'd lighten my load in any way possible.

"There's a trail up ahead," Gus said. "We should be able to go up that face and cut over into the tree line just above the camp."

"Right behind you."

It was noon before we reached the ridge over the camp and the Texas sun was directly above us. I was fine on the level and slight inclines but felt my weakness when the grade increased. The pack was rubbing against my wounds, which didn't feel all too good, either.

We dropped our packs to the ground and sat, wiping the sweat from our faces with hands that were dirty from scrambling up the loose rocks on the climb. My legs were screaming at me to stop, grab a beer, and not move for a few hours. Instead I had some water and acetaminophen.

"You know what sucks more than that hike up here?"

"What?" Gus said.

"Knowing we have to hike back down."

"True but at least it will be downhill. Watch your water. We'll need enough to make it back."

My head was back draining a sixteen-ounce bottle into my mouth. I stopped and put the cap back on with only a few sips left inside. Gus climbed to his feet and stepped to the edge of the ridge below the line of trees giving us shade and looked down into the valley.

"See anything?"

"Got a good view of the camp." He raised the binoculars to his eyes. "There's the car. Silver Chevy Impala."

"No sign of Clem?"

"Not yet."

I pulled my pack over to me, opened the front pouch, and took out a black Motorola walkie-talkie and turned it on. I went from channel to channel listening for any activity but heard only the chirps when it changed frequencies.

We took turns napping to stay fresh, me first then Gus, in one-hour shifts. We had some granola bars he'd brought and the two backpacks had half a dozen MRE's, or meals-ready-to-eat, each.

I was on my second watch and slowly eating half a protein bar while Gus slept with his head on a backpack farther up in the trees where the sun was mostly blocked. I clicked through the channels on the radio every few minutes.

The beeping from Gus's watch alerted me that my turn to rest was coming. I wrapped the protein bar up and put it in my backpack and raised the binoculars to scan the camp before trying to sleep. I worked my way from the east end of the camp to the west and finally the silver car. As I pulled the binoculars away from my eyes, a flash of light entered the lenses from above the camp and I pulled them close again.

Working my view up the incline on the southwest side

of the camp, I saw nothing but trees. Then another flash of light. I centered in on where the light had emitted from and looked for signs of life. After two minutes it flashed again.

"Gus, get up."

"I'm coming. I'm coming," he grunted.

"I think there's someone on the hill on the other side of the camp."

"Could be scouts out for a hike."

I aimed the binoculars back down to the camp. "I never took a full head count but it looks like everyone is still working." Pointing the binoculars back up at the trees again I searched for the flash of light.

Gus sat beside me with the other pair of binoculars. "Show me where."

I described features of the hill more than a mile away and got Gus looking at the same area I was.

"I don't see any—" He paused. "There it is."

"Yup. Saw it, too"

"Always in the same spot?"

"No. Seems to have moved northwest, maybe fifty or sixty feet from the first time I saw it."

"So probably not something sparkly hanging on a branch," Gus said.

"Nope. Definitely moving."

Gus looked up the valley to the right. "Mostly downhill for us heading farther in. Should be able to hit the floor by sundown then make camp."

"You want to give chase?"

"Why'd we come up here?" Gus said.

"We don't even know if it's Clem."

CHAPTER 21

The walk down the ridge of the mountain wasn't much easier. Searching for solid footfalls on a decline is trickier than heading up and we both slipped several times when rocks that looked secure gave way. I was afraid to reach back and touch the bandages over my knife wounds for fear I'd come back with bloody fingers.

We stopped for water breaks regularly and would pull out a pair of binoculars to scan the rise to our west for any sign of the flashing light, seeing it only one more time, one hour after setting out.

"Sun's getting low," Gus said. "It's not at the right angle to cast any reflections. We probably won't see it again today."

"So we're flying blind now. Best we can do is keep moving on an intercept course toward where we think it was headed."

Gus moved out and I fell in behind him again. As the sun began to dip behind the farthest hill, we reached the bottom of the valley. The flatter ground had us making more forward progress but the diminishing light made it harder to see low vegetation that would tangle our feet up.

Curiosity got the best of me and I ran my hand between my back and the backpack and it came back with a small smear of blood. Nothing compared to the day before, but still didn't make me feel confident being in the middle of the mountains with two bleeding wounds.

The temperature dropped rapidly. We rolled two sleeping bags out and Gus made a small fire for warmth once the sun was gone. He took a pair of binoculars and nothing else and walked west from our campsite into the darkness.

I sat beside the fire, feeling more vulnerable than I preferred. My skin was coated with the dried salty sweat from the half day of hiking through the mountains in ninety-degree temperatures and the quick fifteen degree drop bristled my skin and raised the hair on my arms and neck.

It wasn't true that I failed camping in scouts. I simply refused to go. I never understood the desire to become one with nature and sleep on the hard ground with bugs and wild animals all around. I like my bed, my kitchen, and sleeping next to Eva. Clem has probably slept as many nights on the ground as he has on a bed, still regularly goes on camping trips by himself from a couple nights to a full month in the Sierras once.

It wasn't my first time in the wild or even in desert conditions. Eight years ago I was on FBI assignment with the Joint Terrorism Task Force and spent six weeks on the ground in Afghanistan. The temperature was unbearable and I witnessed the toughest soldiers drop from heat stroke during the days. I was sent to investigate the stories of an Al-Qaeda cell that was training for another attack on America, and Washington D.C. specifically. I had a dozen troops to guide and protect me in the harsh conditions and an Afghani handler that was trusted by the Army.

Four weeks into my stay I was in the third of four Humvees rolling through the desert to trace down a lead I'd received from Langley when the handler detonated a suicide vest inside the second vehicle. Only the gunner in the back of the truck survived and that was without his hearing and minus three fingers. My truck turned to the right as the blast occurred. Glass and shrapnel pierced the side of the poorly armored vehicle. I was sitting between two soldiers. The boy on my left, barely old enough to enlist, received the brunt of the shrapnel, leaving his helmet cracked in two and his left arm chopped up like fresh deli meat.

Gus walked quietly back into the campsite and sat on the sleeping bag across from mine. "There's smoke from another campfire about half a mile away," he said. "Looks like it's being dispersed to avoid being seen, probably under a tree or some kind of makeshift wind breaker so it isn't a single column of smoke rising up."

"Should we get closer?"

"Might be worth a shot," Gus said.

Our fire was small and Gus covered it with dirt to put it out. We moved into the darkness, him a few steps ahead of me. Walking seemed easy now with no backpack and the cool night air on my skin. My wounds hurt but it was a relief not having the pack rub against them with every step.

It was further than Gus had thought, the distances at night much harder to gauge with landmarks turned to shadows. After twenty-five minutes of walking I saw Gus's fist come into the air.

We stopped. We listened. I could smell the burned wood of a campfire. I couldn't hear anything, which in itself was unsettling. No insects or animals were making their nocturnal sounds.

Gus used hand signals, not risking his voice carrying across the desert floor.

Twenty feet. He'll go left. I'll go right. Keep a watch behind you.

He went in motion and disappeared into the scrub. I moved in the other direction. I saw his plan, to move to either side of the campfire he'd seen, then meet on the other side.

The isolation was immediate. I knew Gus was not far away. He'd hear me if I snapped my fingers. But he was invisible and the night surrounded me. I became overly aware of my own breathing and the loud beating of my heart in my ears. Each step brought the risk of noise, a cracked stick or bumping a rock that skipped along the dry ground.

I stopped and knelt down, looking out across a small clearing, maybe ten feet across. A sleeping bag was laid out on the ground. To the right of it, a small structure, maybe a foot tall, was made of sticks and a piece of stretched canvas, the dim glow of embers in a hole beneath it.

Across the clearing I thought I saw a shadow move, a disturbance in the darkness. Gus, I thought, working his way around the other side. I watched it as closely as I could, strained my eyes to find the outline, a shape to identify it as Gus.

The smell of sweat hit my nose. I froze for the moment it took to process if it was my own stink, then I felt the heat behind me. As a hand came to my mouth, pulling my head back, an arm came around my body, trapping my holstered gun and pinning my arms. I struggled but was being turned and lowered, my legs buckling under me.

Then warm, moist air hit my ear and a quiet raspy voice whispered. "What the fuck took you so long."

CHAPTER 22

"Hubble is here," Clem said.

We'd moved his camp to ours and sat in a tight group on the ground to keep our voices down. The events of the previous week were shared over a bottle of Jamesons he'd brought with him, passed around in an endless flow of whiskey.

While Gus and I looked like we were out for a hike, Clem looked as if he belonged there. His dark skin glowed with sweat reflecting off of him from the light of the small fire. The Army green T-shirt he wore was worn and dirty from a week in the desert. He smelled of the wild. I tried to not sit too close to him.

"Here?" I said.

"Makes sense. The purchases at the Army surplus store and REI," Gus said.

"You've seen him?" I said.

"Early in the day," Clem said. "He was working along the hill, same route you two took."

"So it was you on the other ridge, the reflections we saw?" I said.

"It was. Needed to get you moving. You two are slow as shit."

"Blame me." I raised my shirt to show the two gauze pads over the knife wounds on my back, both spotted with dried blood. "Souvenirs from meeting a few of Hubble's thugs."

Clem looked at the bandages and shook his head. "Little guy, moves really damn fast?"

"You know him?" I said.

"I know him. He's Nepali. He was working as a mercenary in Afghanistan and Ortiz practically adopted him," Clem said. "Did it feel like someone tapping you back there, no pain?"

"Exactly. Hit me quick two times, spun me around. Didn't realize I was cut until the next morning."

"That's a Gurkha Kukri," Clem said. "Nasty knives. Standard issue for the Nepalese Army. Lucky for you, looks like it was on the smaller size. The bigger ones would have left you in two pieces."

"However big, it did a job on me. Any deeper and Eva said I would have bled out within minutes."

"Sounds like he only wanted to hurt you."

"Hopefully he never wants to do any worse," I said.

"Is Hubble tracking you?" Gus said.

"He's trying. I've doubled back and changed trails so

many times it left him dizzy," Clem said. "He's camped over at the base of the south ridge right now. For Army, he's not much of an outdoorsman."

"He was Army ROTC and went in as an officer," I said. "Except for the time at Fenty, he's driven a desk his entire career."

"What do you wanna do about him?" Gus said.

"Was waiting for you two to catch up then figure that out. Don't think you have enough on him to hold him, aside from the pot."

We all thought and drank whiskey. The insects were loud again, used to our presence, accepting us into their world. Looking up, I felt the sky was the biggest I'd seen since my time in Afghanistan, the wide open expanse of blackness dotted with bright stars that disappear once you are around any form of man made light sources.

"Would be good to get him out of the way for a while so we can figure things out and track down Ortiz," Gus said.

"Good luck with that. The eighteen months I was at Fenty I never met Ortiz once. As far as I know, nobody had," Clem said. "He's a ghost."

"You sure it's not just Hubble? Some boss character he made up to keep people in line?"

"Hubble's not smart enough for that. He's no leader," Clem said.

"Did they try to get you to work for them, is that how you got mixed up in this?" Gus said.

Clem downed a shot of whiskey and poked at the small fire between us. The flames were built in a hole a foot deep and a piece of canvas was stretched on three sticks to disperse what little smoke came off the fire.

"I did work for them," Clem said.

Gus and I looked at each other.

"Hubble approached me several times trying to get me interested. They really wanted someone from the Rangers, an experienced soldier to help with the planning. They lost two guys, nineteen and twenty years old, in a stupid accident when they got cocky on a drop off."

"He told you this while trying to recruit you?" I said.

"No. I'd heard about the boys getting shot," Clem said. "Army wrote it off as an attack on a patrol. After I was in they told me everything."

"Why did you do it?" Gus said.

"Trust me, I didn't want to. But the third time they came for me, they had some information that I didn't really want getting out. Said they'd make sure the whole base, including brass, heard it."

"This have anything to do with your sealed juvie record?" I said.

Clem looked up at me and nodded. "You've done good. Yeah. That damn record should have been destroyed years earlier, but the Texas system is so backed up that files are sitting around ten years after they're supposed to be shredded. Wasn't hard for them to find it and get access. Then they had all they needed to hang me if I refused to work with them."

"Is the record that bad?" I said.

He shook his head. "Wasn't good. I was mixed up with the wrong guys. They decided to knock over a liquor store. Turns out they had no idea what they were doing. The shop owner got shot and died a week later. Three of us were picked up based on descriptions. I gladly gave up the other two. So between the possible manslaughter charge and needing to get away from them, I chose the Army when given a choice."

"Then when you found out they had that info on you, you agreed." I said.

"Not before talking to the JAG on base," Clem said. "I told him everything I knew and what I suspected. Gave him dates of shipments that had gone missing and logs of who had been on the convoys. He ate it up. He wanted them. It was a career maker, woulda sent him straight to D.C. and end up a federal judge a decade earlier than he'd planned."

"You wanted to bring them down," Gus said.

"I did. What I didn't know was they already had the JAG in their pocket," Clem said. "Turned out he liked boys and at that time in the Army, in a war zone, it would have ruined him. He told Hubble within an hour of our meeting. Instead of getting the shit beat out of me and probably killed by our common Nepali friend, I volunteered."

"You actually did it then, worked with them?" I said.

"Just once. I rode shotgun and looked tough while they made the deal."

"And after that?" I said.

"I got my unit transferred. A series of attacks happened at Bagram and we went to deal with those."

"Why is he after you now?" Gus said.

"He just transferred into Fort Hood six months ago," Clem said. "We passed each other in a hallway and he looked like he'd seen a ghost. Was a week later he showed up at my building. Felt more like he was seeing where I was, if I was a risk. Probably a month went by and he came back. Had a new plan, bigger and better and safer than before," he said.

"Marijuana," I said.

"Yup. But just for starters. He said he had a network in place to bring harder stuff across the border from Mexico. Cocaine. Fentanyl. To him, our old deal was still in place. I still belonged to him."

"Where does Leo Ortiz fit in? He still in the picture?" Gus said.

"Oh yeah," Clem said. "And from what Hubble said, sounds like Ortiz is in Killeen calling the shots. But there's no one with that name at Fort Hood except a few privates straight out of boot camp."

"I have a thought," Gus said. "Let's get Hubble arrested."

CHAPTER 23

Stiff bodies made walking first thing in the morning difficult. The aftereffects of whiskey didn't help either. A blister had formed and broken on the bottom of my right foot and I tried to keep from limping away from the sharp pain with every step. There was no fresh blood when I checked my wounds, but still I replaced the gauze and had Gus tape it in place. I was running low on acetaminophen and rationed down to two pills at a time.

The morning went from cool and damp from the light layer of dew that had settled on the plants to hot and dry within a few minutes of setting out on the trail. The sun was behind us as it continued its inevitable rise into the sky, causing Gus and me to take our shirts off and wrap them around the backs of our necks to avoid the sunburn that would come too quickly. Clem had a hat with a mesh floppy brim and I was tempted to wrestle him for it. But I'd smelled him the night before after being in the desert for nearly a week without a shower and I didn't want to get that close to him.

We'd stop for water and food breaks then push forward. Clem led us, ever the Ranger. Just past noon he slowed as he reached a slight rise in the ground and held his fist up in the air to tell us to stop. He lowered to a knee and pulled binoculars out. After getting a look in the distance, he motioned for us to join him.

"Straight ahead and just to the left of that small cliff area." Clem pointed with a flat hand and we followed with our own binoculars. "Under a small grove of trees."

"It's a car," I said.

"Hubble's car," Clem said.

We'd discussed the plan the night before and knew our parts. Clem was most at risk and would remain farthest from the vehicle. Gus and I moved on until we were fifty yards from the white Honda Pilot. We searched every direction with the binoculars, as Clem was doing from far behind us. Single clicks on the walkie-talkies told us it was clear.

Gus moved out. He admitted I was the better shot and wanted me to cover him. All I had was my Glock, but I was accurate with it even at distance, plus I could close the gap quickly if needed.

I watched him through the lenses, scanning left and right to look for any other motion. Another click from the walkie, all clear. Gus arrived at the car and waited until we gave him another click that it was good to continue.

The car key was found on the third try, on top of the back left tire. No hiker wants to carry their keys with them and risk losing them in the wilderness. He unlocked the back hatch and was out of view for half a minute before closing it, wiping the handle down, and returning the key to the tire. I continued scanning until he was back with me and we stopped often while retreating to check our six, the clicks continuing to come from Clem.

The next step was put into motion with a call on the radio. Clem finished his short conversation and then we waited. It was more than an hour later that we heard the first sounds, then the growling got louder. The ATV came into view and Gus stood and waved it down. It sped up to our hiding spot and the driver took off his helmet.

The man from the Boy Scout camp looked at us and nodded. "Sorry, guys."

"It's all good," I said.

"Eddie, Gus, this is Zach," Clem said. "He was one of my Rangers until he settled down to civilian life. Now he runs the Boy Scout camp here when he isn't fishing in the gulf."

Clem pulled his pack on and said his goodbyes, which for him meant saying "Later" as he climbed onto the back of the ATV. It took off, sending dirt flying into the air, on a long route through the open valley to go back to the scout camp.

Gus and I watched for motion along the far hill. The ATV made a trail of dust in the air throughout the valley. We turned and headed back up the trail. An hour later we came across two older Boy Scouts sitting on ATVs under trees at the bottom of the north hill.

Everything depended on Hubble seeing Clem's ride through the valley and heading back toward the scout camp. We needed him to get out on the highway.

The scouts drove us back to the camp. It was deserted. Wheelbarrows and shovels were left where they'd last been used.

"Everyone's gone up top." One of the drivers pointed to the highest ridge of the state park. He was barely eighteen, probably, but one of the senior boys at the camp. "High ground, safest place. Only a few of us know what's happening, the older ones. The rest think it was just an emergency evacuation drill in case of flooding."

The Impala was gone. Clem got here before us and had left, as planned. The scouts drove us down to our SUV and we followed suit. Coming down out of the park our phones found signals again and both started beeping with text messages and voicemails that had been floating in the air waiting to land. I had a text from the club telling me a band had canceled for Saturday night, two from Shelley wanting me to call her, one from Eva with a kissy face and an eggplant emoji, and a voicemail letting me know I could get a great rate on a home equity loan by calling them back immediately.

Half an hour later we stopped to fill the tank and buy some much needed junk food. Even Gus went through three packs of Hostess chocolate donuts as we headed toward the highway.

"Grab your walkie," Gus said. "Put it on channel 21."

I did. "Clem's radio silent until we know Hubble is secured."

"I know," Gus said. "Just humor me."

It was twenty minutes before a sound came from the small speaker. First it was a crackling noise, then words, broken and distorted as they were being reassembled by circuits and wires, then the voice came through clearly.

"Who is that?" I said.

"That's Hubble. I put the other walkie under his seat with the button held down by a rubber band."

"Special Agent Gus Ramirez," I said. "You are a genius."

Hubble made a phone call that ended quickly from bad cell connection. A few minutes later and another attempt.

"It's me. I'm headed back and think he's ahead of me."

We could only hear his side of the conversation.

"Someone picked him up on a four-wheeler. I saw him, okay? I can't stay in the damn desert forever. He went toward the camp then his car was gone when I drove back over to check."

I adjusted the volume as the signal faded.

"Just… just… do whatever the hell you want. I'm on the highway trying to catch up to him."

"He doesn't sound happy," I said.

"I'll run him off the goddamn road if I have to."

The call ended.

"Think it was Ortiz?" Gus said.

"Had to be."

"If we had his number we could do a phone records check and get Ortiz's number."

"Then could easily locate him," I said.

"But we don't."

"So we can't."

Gus had the cruise control set at 80 miles per hour. It was hard not to put music on so we could hear the walkie.

"We were parked on the east side of the park, right," Gus said.

"Yup."

"And Hubble would have been on the west side."

"Northwest, true."

"We think he got on the road before us, right?"

"It's our guess. Even with the ATV ride back, he should have been closer to his car than we were."

"Guess this makes sense then," Gus said.

"What?"

"Hubble is behind us and about to pass."

The white Honda appeared to be pushing its limits to pass us. The dark tint on the Explorer allowed us some anonymity in looking over at him.

"He looks pissed," Gus said.

"He's gonna look more pissed soon."

I hit dial on my phone and talked for less than a minute and hung up.

"All set?"

"Yup. And even better than we thought. Speed up, don't lose him. I want to see this."

Gus pushed his speed and kept the Honda within a quarter mile. A few minutes later Hubble's speed dropped as we hit the first signs for the small town ahead of us.

"He's still going 70 headed in to Fort Stockton," Gus said.

"Perfect. Gives them good reason then."

We'd made the first slight bend to the left when the white Ford Taurus came out from the Walmart parking lot and fell in behind Hubble, blue lights flashing.

"Here we go," I said.

Swearing came through the speaker on the walkie and a thumping sound I guessed was him hitting the steering wheel.

The cruiser matched speed and was six feet off the bumper of the Honda. We were ten car lengths back.

"He's not stopping," Gus said.

"Would be crazy not to," I said.

"Right? I know I don't wanna piss off small town cops."

Hubble's voice came through the walkie again.

"I have police behind me, pulling me over."

Quiet while he listened.

"No, it's not state troopers. Some small ass town in the middle of nowhere. Local PD."

A second cruiser screamed past us and fell in behind the other, the Honda still steady at 70 in the right lane.

"What? You gotta be able to do something. Call Hendrickson at state police and have him call the sheriff or chief of police or whatever the hell they have here."

The sirens came on and the second cruiser sped up to cut Hubble off.

"Fuck. I gotta stop. Just call someone, okay?"

The brake lights came on. Hubble slowed and pulled to the wide shoulder of the highway running through town. Gus pulled off and stopped far enough back to not be noticed. With his plates not visible, the Explorer blended in enough or looked like back up unmarked police waiting in case the officer needed help.

A tall, round man in a white uniform shirt and tan cowboy hat climbed out of the cruiser, right hand on the grip of his service pistol. A matching officer in size and shape came from the front of Hubble's car.

Even through the closed window in the Honda, we could hear the police yelling through the walkie.

"Open your door and get out of the vehicle, hands on top of your head!"

"This is getting good," Gus said.

"Where's the popcorn?"

Hubble complied. The moment he was clear of the door, one of the officers took his raised elbow and spun his body into the side of the SUV.

A third officer showed up in a white F-150 with official markings and a light bar. His cowboy hat was bigger than the first two.

"Wanna bet that's the chief?" I said.

They let Hubble turn and talk. Through his hand motions and mannerisms I imagined what he was saying, that he didn't see the speed limit sign, he was distracted, anything to just get a ticket written and get on his way.

One of the officers opened the back doors. A backpack was taken out and dropped on the ground after quick inspection. Finally a deputy raised the rear hatch.

"You know, Texans may love their guns," Gus said. "But a bag full of automatic weapons and ammunition will still get your ass arrested."

"Not to mention the three hand grenades," I said.

"What the hell was Clem doing with hand grenades anyway?"

"I don't know, but I'm glad he had them."

A second officer was called to the rear of the car as the bag was opened, then both stepped back to the side, weapons drawn and aimed.

Hubble was thrown face down on the ground, handcuffs slapped on his wrists.

"When I called my trooper friend he said he'd get these local guys to do the stop in case Hubble was connected."

"Sounds like he was."

"I'll be sure to tell them to check into this Hendrickson person," I said. "Let's get out of here."

"Let's."

CHAPTER 24

I slid the magazine in until it made a satisfying click. Seventeen bullets at my disposal. I grabbed the top of the slide with my left hand, pulled it back, released it, and it flew forward. The first bullet moved into the chamber, ready to fire. They got so many things wrong in movies, when actors ride the slide both directions with their hand. I'd seen fresh recruits at Quantico do that, lawyers and language specialists who applied to the FBI without ever having shot a gun and found themselves crawling through mud and firing handguns and rifles. Not letting go of that slide was a sure way to lose a large chunk of skin, not to mention the possibility of a misfire due to the round not seating properly.

My forefinger stretched out above the trigger guard, always extended until time to shoot. Weapon raised, barrel down range. The popping and banging around me were a blur through my ear protection. They were sounds I'd heard too many times to take notice of. The open air range helped, too. Not like shooting indoor with every blast echoing off the cement walls. To my right someone pumped out ten rounds from a .45 in five seconds. Other shooting stopped as people stared at the idiot blowing through ammo thinking he looked cool.

The target was at 100-yards. Long for a 9mm for most people to be accurate. I thought of Gus working through the desert scrub the day before, his back to me, his life in my hands. I hadn't shot long range in a while.

Self defense or handgun combat is within five yards. Fifteen feet. That's not very far. Even the most inexperienced shooter had a good chance of landing a shot at that short distance. Two to the chest, one to the head was the standard. It was the Mozambique Drill, or the Failure Drill, depending on who you asked. If the two in the chest didn't stop them, one to the head definitely will. Story had it a Rhodesian mercenary in the Mozambican War of Independence had come around a corner and found himself a few yards from an enemy guerilla. He raised his pistol and put two shots in the man's chest, on either side of the sternum, but the man was still advancing. The mercenary raised his aim and put one shot through the base of the guerilla's neck, severing the spinal cord and dropping him to the ground. A shooting instructor who heard the story named it the Mozambique Drill and began to teach it to SWAT teams around the country.

I aimed. The thick paper target with the silhouette of a man was stapled to a piece of cardboard, moving ever so slightly in the open air. Adjusted. Compensated for the crosswind. No matter how light the breeze, a bullet's path can be affected.

Inhale. Hold. Exhale.

I lowered my gun without firing, sat it on the shelf beside me, and tapped a button on my phone to start the timer and turned away.

Down the hill and on the other side of a chain link fence, picnic tables were spread out across the grounds of the large shooting range. It was a weekend activity, something fun to do. Children played nearby, the ones who weren't targeting .22's and .30-06's at 60 yards to practice for the next deer or squirrel hunting season. People ate lunch, talked, and enjoyed the day. It's a sport to most of them. A game. Maybe they hunt. Maybe they compete. Maybe they think they'll be the one to stop a shooter in a restaurant or the mall. Maybe they'll be the one who gets killed trying to stop a shooter.

A man several positions down from me had five pistols, a huge revolver and an AR-15 with every accessory available attached to it. He was standing with one foot up on the stool, showing off his collection. Something told me there was a lot more guns back home.

I own one gun. My Glock 17. I know it inside and out. It has thirty-four parts. The trigger travels 12.5 millimeters. Today over a hundred rounds will go through it and at home it will be cleaned, reloaded, and returned to the floor safe until tomorrow.

Until recently I carried a .40 caliber. It was heavier and ammunition was more expensive. I switched to the 9mm for weight and convenience and because shooting off 200 rounds in an hour didn't make my arms hurt. With 124-grain jacketed hollow point rounds I could still stop most people coming at me with a pair of well placed shots.

Finding Clem was only the beginning. Hubble will clear jail in Fort Stockton. Ortiz is still a ghost. I won't leave home without my gun until this mess is cleaned up.

You don't find yourself shooting 100-yards with a handgun very often in self defense. Generally it's more up close and personal.

The timer on my phone chimed. Before the first beeps ended, I'd turned and the Glock was back in my right hand, aimed, adjusted for wind, and a single 9mm bullet was released from the barrel. The next round loaded into the chamber when the slide flew forward.

I picked up the binoculars and looked down range. The hole was two inches off center to left. It would still be a deadly blow, but it wasn't perfect.

I began again.

CHAPTER 25

Eva was still asleep as I dressed. She'd come home from the night shift just after 8:00 a.m., showered, and collapsed into bed. She stayed awake just long enough to ask what had happened, then fell asleep with her hand on my bare chest. As I left the bedroom in the morning she stirred and mumbled a few words.

"Wear your vest."

And she was asleep again.

Gus was outside leaning on his Explorer. He saw my black Kevlar and pulled his on, too, more out of support for me, but it was a good idea considering how the last couple days had gone. He put his T-shirt back on over his and I had a loose fitting button down that covered enough of mine to not be obvious.

He had coffee waiting in the car and we didn't speak

much on the drive to Killeen. His phone rang as we hit city limits and he answered with a button on the steering wheel.

"Ramirez."

"Boss, it's Harper." The voice came through the stereo speakers. "Hubble bounced about fifteen minutes ago. A call came from the capital and the chief of police in Fort Stockton didn't pursue charges."

"Shit," Gus said. "Thanks, Harper." He hung up.

"Stayed in longer than I thought he would," I said.

Gus looked at his watch. "Almost forty-eight hours."

"He's still at least five hours away, so we should be clear."

We parked on the street outside the Hubble house. The curtains were drawn as they had been the other times we were there. The minivan and covered Corvette sat in the carport.

I rang the doorbell and we waited. There were no sounds of children yelling or playing. It was a school day and his wife should be home alone. The door opened.

"Can I help you?"

"Yes, Mrs. Hubble, I'm Special Agent Gus Ramirez with the FBI. I was hoping we could chat with your husband for a few minutes." We wanted in to talk to her but didn't want to be obvious.

She was five-foot-eight and slender, but moved like she meant it, each motion concise and planned. Her hand ran down the edge of the door she held open as she thought.

"He's not here right now. If you wish to leave a business card—"

"Can we speak with you, then?" I said.

Her eyes went to each of us again, taking us in.

"I know you," she said. "I mean, I recognize you."

"We have those kinds of faces," I said.

"No. You two were snooping around my carport a few days ago," she said. "My phone sends me alerts when anyone comes close."

We were busted and there was no reason to deny it.

"Yes, ma'am," I said. "We were."

"Why?" Even in questioning why two strange men were casing her home, she stood relaxed, calm.

"Information from a case brought us to this address," Gus said and glanced toward the street. "Can we come in and talk where it's more private?"

She hesitated, then stepped back and opened the door wide.

"Sure. Come on in."

She offered coffee and we both declined. Gus sat on the edge of a very soft looking chair and she sat on the matching sofa, her arm wrapped around a throw pillow. I stood behind Gus.

"Tell me, why is the FBI knocking on my door wanting to speak with my husband?" She had a pretty smile, just enough teeth showing and her eyes engaged. She was very deliberate.

"Ma'am, we're—" Gus was interrupted.

"Please call me Cady," she said. "I've always hated ma'am."

"Yes, Cady," Gus said. "We're looking into, well, there's no gentle way to say this, a series of murders and attempted murders."

She straightened her back, eyes went wide. "How horrible. Around here? On our street?"

"No, ma'— Cady. One was in San Antonio and two were in Austin," Gus said.

I was happy to let him do the talking. He was the one with the actual badge after all. It let me watch her and look around the room. We needed to know if she knew who her husband really was.

"What do they have to do with Benjamin and me?"

"All of the victims were stationed at Fenty the same time as your husband," Gus said. "We're investigating a connection between them, a criminal connection."

My knees were sore from the hiking, so I moved around to keep from getting stiff, stepping away from the chair where Gus was sitting. A row of framed photographs were lined up in a built in bookcase. A wedding photo, she looked amazing, her arms toned in the sleeveless dress, him in his dress blues. One of each child, and one of them all together. A shelf above was several of Hubble in camouflage with a group of men, all young and fresh out of boot camp.

"What kind of crimes?" Cady said.

"We're still determining that, but appears to be theft of government property."

"In Afghanistan?" she said.

"It seems so," Gus said.

I stepped over to the next shelf, more photos from the Army. Each had smiling, happy soldiers grouped up and I scanned from one to the next. My eyes caught on a photograph and I froze. The hair on my arms raised. I held still and opened my senses, taking in everything I could. Hearing heightened, vision became sharper. I moved slowly as I had been, looking around, and crossed back behind

Gus's chair until I was several feet to his right.

Finally I turned toward her and she was looking at me, her head turned away from Gus, following me. She knew I knew.

Instincts kicked in and motions were smooth and fast. My hand was on my Glock and had it clear of its holster, raised and aimed at Cady Hubble.

I spoke loud and firm. "Hands where I can see them."

She feigned a startled expression as Gus jumped up. His hand pulled his weapon. "What the hell, Eddie?"

Cady had one hand around a pillow, hidden. Her smile dropped and shoulders squared. The confidence and precision I'd seen in her earlier made sense. She was military.

"I suggest you put your weapon down, Mr. Holland, and place it on the table," she said. "You too, Special Agent Ramirez."

When we arrived I never told her my name.

"Eddie, what's happening?" Gus said.

I took a half step forward, my aim not wavering. My finger moved from the trigger guard to the trigger. She saw that small motion.

"I'll only say it one more time," she said. "Weapons on the table."

"Hands where I can see them," I said.

She exhaled loudly and shook her head. "I warned you."

Three shots came through the window behind me, the glass shattering and striking me from behind. In the moment my gun was off aim, her hand came up with a small pistol that had been hidden behind the pillow. I rushed her and moved to the right as she pulled the trigger. I felt the 9mm go through the loose sleeve on my left arm. I hit the sofa hard, landing on top of her, and rolled the large piece of furniture over while working to get an arm around her and a hand out to disable her gun.

Gus had gone to a knee and stayed low, his Sig out while he moved to the window. Three more shots came through, the blasts louder as the shooters moved closer.

"Eddie, we're about to have company," Gus said. "Three men coming fast."

I was on my back and had Cady Hubble in a choke hold but she was strong and wiry. An elbow came down into my ribs. My right arm was extended out, holding her gun hand.

Two loud blasts as Gus fired through the broken front window.

"Now it's two men coming fast," he said.

A gun fight in a residential neighborhood is a dangerous thing. A 9mm round doesn't stop for windows or walls, it keeps going. Wooden studs only slow it down. Sheetrock and siding barely affect it. A bullet can end up three houses down embedded in a refrigerator door, if you are lucky. If you aren't lucky you have a gunshot victim who has no idea what happened.

Her gun hand twisted and broke loose of my grip as she brought it around toward my head. I caught her wrist again but she got a round off that grazed my scalp. I loosened my chokehold with my left, grabbed her shirt and pulled her hard, rolling her body across mine then face down to the floor. With the momentum I threw my leg up and came over on top of her. I grabbed the gun from her hand and struck the barrel across her temple and her body went limp below me.

Like at the range, I'd paid no attention to the shots behind me, allowing me to focus on not dying. I turned on my knee and looked up from behind the overturned sofa. Gus was beside the window exchanging fire with two men outside.

"You done playing around and gonna help now?" he said.

"Sure. What's the situation?"

"One shooter is coming through the door in about five seconds," he said. "I have the other pinned behind a tree in the front yard."

My hand went to my hip but the Glock wasn't there. I looked around on the floor and couldn't see it as two rounds came through the lock on the front door. I ran around the overturned sofa and reached the entry just as the barrel of a HK45 appeared. I grabbed the shooter's wrist with my right hand and pulled across my body, against his joint, until his body came around the corner. My left arm was up and around the near side of his neck, pushing his head away from his hand in a very unnatural position. My hand slipped up onto the HK45 and inside the trigger guard on top of his. Pushing his arm up, I pulled and fired off the six remaining shots into the ceiling.

With the gun empty, his hand released its grip. I grabbed the barrel and spun to strike it into his head. Before the impact, his knee came up into my groin and doubled me over. He struck me in the back of my head with both hands and as I was falling to the floor I heard a single shot and the man's body fell along with me.

"That was my last round so we'd better figure something out quick," Gus said.

I pointed toward the sofa. "My gun—"

He stayed low and ran to find my pistol as I got to my feet, bullets still coming through the open window hitting walls and pictures.

"Where is she?" Gus said.

"What?"

"Where's Cady Hubble?"

I straightened up fast and regretted it immediately, my head hurting, then moved along the wall to the sofa and looked down at the floor. She was gone.

"Must have gone through the back door," Gus said.

I pushed the overturned sofa out of the way and found my Glock, checked the magazine, fifteen rounds remained. I'd only gotten two shots off before dropping my weapon.

"Hear that?" I said.

"The shooting stopped," Gus said.

We ran down opposite walls and looked through the tattered curtain as a silver SUV sped away.

"Shit."

"What the hell just happened? Why'd you draw on her?" Gus said.

I went to the bookshelves and found the photograph on the floor in front of it, the glass now broken, and handed it to Gus. Benjamin and Cady Hubble were smiling, his arm around her, both wearing Army fatigues.

"She was in the Army, too?" Gus said.

"Look at her name."

Gus's eyes moved to the sewed-on patch over her left breast in the photograph and read it out loud.

"Ortiz."

CHAPTER 26

I made my third drive down I-35 through Austin in an hour, exiting at a different road each time, while Eva grew more irritated in the passenger seat. I knew this because she hadn't spoken in at least twenty minutes. She understood it was for her own safety, but she'd had to call in sick for the night shift at the hospital and was now being relocated to a hotel. We were in a small Nissan SUV borrowed from the FBI motor pool, something that had been acquired for those times you don't want to be rolling in a vehicle that screams law enforcement like a Charger or Explorer.

"Why can't I have my cellphone?" She broke her silence.

"Because they could track it."

"Who is they?"

"Better if you don't know."

"Is it that Hubble guy?"

I exhaled loudly. Sometimes I wished I didn't tell her everything about my cases, but she's just too good at finding the details I miss sometimes.

"Yes. But forget that name. You never heard it."

"Right," she said. "I remember my first grade babysitter's boyfriend's mother's name."

"I'm just trying to protect you."

"I don't need protecting."

"From these people, you do." My sister and her family had to be put into FBI protection after a case I was on put them in direct danger. The night of Eva and my first date ended with her being attacked. I'd put too many people in danger, I wasn't letting it happen again.

"Please. For me," I said. "Hopefully for just a night or two."

She was already checked in under a fake name and the keycards were in my pocket. No need to stop at the front desk and risk acting suspicious or scared. After checking the room out, I opened the door to the adjoining room and knocked on the second door. It opened and Clem was standing there in nothing but a Dallas Cowboys T-shirt, a pair of boxers, and only one leg.

"Well that's a sight to make eyes sore," I said.

"Screw you, too," he said.

"You remember Eva?"

She stepped over to the door and hugged Clem, who balanced perfectly on one leg while doing so.

As they began to catch up there was a knock on the door and I answered it. Gus came in with a grocery bag without saying anything to me because he didn't need to, then greeted Clem and Eva. He sat the bag down on the end of the bed and pulled out two six-packs of Shiner Bohemian Black Lager.

Clem took one while I grabbed a bottle opener.

"Black lager," Clem said. "You get this because I'm black?"

"No, asshole. I got it because I saw a case of it in your fridge at home."

He laughed. "Yeah. It's good shit."

Gus pulled the curtain back an inch and looked down into the parking lot.

"You clean getting here?" Clem said.

"Sure as we can be. Toured every corner of the county on the way," Gus said.

"Same," I said, and Eva rolled her eyes.

Clem nodded. "Anything new? I'm getting tired of sitting here. Was happier wandering around the mountains."

"At least we know where you are now," I said.

We told him about the shootout at the Hubble house.

"His wife?"

"Leocadia Ortiz is her real name," I said.

"Leo Ortiz," Clem said. "Damn."

"Yup. Then after she married seems like she used the second part of her name, Cady," I said.

"She got to Fenty before the date range of our records," Gus said. "They married on base and she changed her name, so by the time we see her, she's Hubble."

"Explains why we never found Ortiz in the data," I said. "We never asked William Jennings if he knew Hubble's wife, because we didn't know she was there."

"When we were at Fenty, I knew he was married, think we all did," Clem said. "But never realized she was Ortiz, of course. Where are they now?"

"We don't know," I said.

"What about their kids?" Clem said.

"Seems Ortiz went straight from a shootout to their youngest's daycare and Hubble got the older two from school," Gus said. "They were gone before we ever got cars there to watch for them."

The six pack went quickly. The minibar was raided. We talked about the Hubbles, getting anything Clem could remember from the days at Fenty. He remembered most of the people on our list from D.O.D. Random thoughts would be voiced, anything we thought might connect some points together.

"Ortiz is very connected," Gus said. "We have to be careful who we trust."

"But it doesn't seem like she has anyone in the FBI," I said. "Or you would have gotten a call by now."

"Not yet, at least," Gus said.

I parked the borrowed Nissan near my old apartment, hid the key under the seat, and began my run as I had so many times down that street. Apartment buildings lined both sides, some nicer than others. After tapping a button on my phone to start music to my earbuds, the playlist of Guy Clark songs I'd curated over the years began. Most people like something upbeat when running, and I do too sometimes. Other times I need the stories of west Texas as a background. A notification for a text message from Shelley was on the screen. I dismissed it.

There are times you need the familiar. The road you know, the sights around you, the music playing too loudly in your ears. I picked up the pace and cleared the first corner and headed for Zilker Park. Each song took me somewhere else emotionally. When "My Favorite Picture of You" came on it was impossible to not think of Eva. "Old Friends" was Gus and Clem. It was strange to think that these songs written by a man many years older, now gone from this world, would resonate each and every time I heard them.

The park was busy for a weekday. I ended up on the dirt sides of the trail to pass other runners, moms pushing strollers, and the random walkers with their hands behind their backs staring off at the river and downtown across the water. I can understand that. Austin has an effect on me, a gravitational pull. There was never any doubt I'd end up back here, though I didn't expect it to be as soon as it was.

My years in D.C. had been good in a stressful and a slowly-killing-my-soul kind of way. I'd thrown myself into my work with no regard for personal time or self care. I'd stopped running. Lunch was whatever was near the office. Gus came to visit once when he was working out of the New York field office for a few months and the look on his face when he saw me said everything. That was maybe six months before I took my leave of absence.

I turned left to go past Barton Springs, sweat coating my skin. Every corner of the park, of the city, had multiple memories associated with them. Gus and I spent many hours in the water at Barton Springs, swimming laps and playing tag when younger, goofing off when older, trying to get the attention of the girls who sat on the edge, only their legs dangling into the water. I don't think we were ever successful in doing anything other than embarrassing ourselves in front of them.

I'd come to the far end of the park and wasn't ready to head home, so I cut back and crossed the bridge at South

Lamar into downtown and slowed my pace to last the extra several miles I would do with the detour. A right turn on 6th Street and the sidewalks were mostly empty. Tonight would be different once all the bars and clubs opened and the sounds of the live music that made the city famous spilled out into the street. A few blocks down I passed my bar, Buddy's Music Parlor, and kept going.

Finally I let myself think about Hubble and Ortiz. I'd hesitated. I knew she had a gun under the pillow, but I hesitated. I've never shot, or hit, a woman before, but have never thought I'd have any problem doing so if it were my life or hers. My mind moved around that room where we'd stood, my gun aimed at her, ready to fire. Photographs lined bookshelves, images of her three children. Did being a mother offset being a criminal? Is that why I didn't shoot, for the sake of those kids?

A right on Congress with the capitol building behind me and I crossed the river again. There's a point in a long run when the exhaustion leaves you and your body feels light. It's that euphoria runners talk about that most people never experience. As I slowed down to stop at the small SUV I felt as if I could turn around and do the entire run again, but I knew I had just put in at least twelve miles.

I pulled my phone out and tapped to stop the music as another notification from Shelley popped up. I went to clear it then tapped to open it instead and read the short message.

Call me. Now. Dad's in hospice.

CHAPTER 28

The house was set back off the road, rows of trees on either side of the drive that were almost artificially green from being watered daily in the dry climate. I parked and sat for a moment, not ready to go in. I saw Shelley's minivan in my mirror and hoped her husband wasn't with her. Not that I didn't like him, I just didn't care for him much.

I'd ignored her texts and voicemails. That was on me. Cases don't wait. Bad people don't put their plans on hold because you have family issues to attend to. But there are times you have to jump off the speeding truck and take care of your own. My dad even found his way home from a deployment when Shelley got sick once. She had been eight, maybe nine years old. For a time the doctors weren't sure what it was or if she'd make it. And he showed up, still carrying his duffel he'd traveled with from another country, and sat at the hospital for five days until her fever broke. I'd failed Shelley by not listening, not answering, not paying attention.

I signed in at the front desk and walked down the center hall. They'd made the place try to feel as much like a home as they could, but the purpose of the building was obvious in the hospital-like feel. One room had four large industrial washing machines and dryers, bundles of white sheets piled up in a cart waited to be fed through. The large living room had sofas and recliners in three separate sitting areas, a sign of the multiple families that would be here at the same time using the six different patient rooms. Plaques with names of philanthropists and donor companies were mounted on anything that cost more than the nonprofit could afford to buy on their own.

A few people were in one of the sitting areas. A small boy watched cartoons on the television while grownups sat on the sofa not talking. A kitchen in the corner had fresh cookies on a large platter, the scent of the melted chocolate chips floating in the air just above the smell of disinfectant.

I found Room Number 4 and stopped at the door. A piece of paper was inside a metal frame with a typed name printed on it.

Edward Holland.

It had been too long since I'd seen him, since visiting his nursing home and sitting with him in his silence.

Before I could push the door, it opened and Shelley almost walked into me.

"You're here." My sister's arms went around me and held tight, head laying flat on my chest. I could feel her body shake as she cried.

"How is he?"

"Not good." Her voice was muffled against me. She pulled back, hands on my arms as she looked at me. A smile worked through the sadness. "Go."

She gently pushed me toward the open door as she walked away down the hall, her arms going around her own body in the absence of anyone else's to hold in that moment.

We were as close as a brother and sister could be. There were the rough times growing up, of course, and times I'm sure we hated each other. But all the adolescent and young adult angst had faded when we matured and we realized we needed each other. I'd put her and her family in danger with my work and in my efforts to keep that from happening again, I found myself not seeing her as often as I should. Her children loved me, and I loved them. Her husband is another subject.

The room was large. One wall had floor to ceiling windows overlooked a central grassy area with benches and a small playground structure. The sliding glass door was open a few feet, allowing fresh air in on the cooler Texas day. Two girls were sitting at the top of the slide together, laughing and playing some childhood game with clapping and large arm movements. A woman sat on a bench looking out at the low trees that separated the house from a city park.

My father was the last thing I looked at, needing those few extra moments before being engulfed in that emotion. The practical side of me, the logistical, first wanted to see every corner, each exit and entrance. When I could put it off no longer I stepped to his bed and looked down.

His eyes were closed in unrestful sleep. A mask was on his face with air being pushed into him to help breathing, a CPAP machine only for comfort. Nothing is done to prolong life here, only make you comfortable. The entire building, the mission of this place, was to allow you to die in dignity, as much as one can. It loses the overly sterile and impersonal feel of a hospital and brings in the bare essentials of home. The nurses experience death three times a week, a new family coming in to take the place of the last to grieve through the final days or weeks as a disease runs its course and achieves its goal.

The Alzheimer's had taken his brain years ago. The cancer that came last year destroyed his body. His skin was loose and he didn't look like himself. Even as a man ages, he retains his looks, is recognizable, but with years added. The disease comes in and causes weight loss, muscle deterioration, and changes your face and your body. I took his hand in mine and it no longer had that sense of strength, a hand that had fired so many rounds of ammunition in the Army, fought hand-to-hand in training, and struck my ass as a child.

A few photos from his nursing home were on the shelves, images from the Army, Shelley and I as children, her kids. To the right was one of me from the day I graduated Quantico, standing next to the Director, shaking his hand. I knew she had brought that, of course, but seeing it made me feel good.

For years in the nursing home they would say to talk to him, that he was in there somewhere and could hear me and understand. I never fully believed them but had done so anyway. He'd become my confidant, my free psychiatrist that only listened and offered no commentary. I'd confessed things from childhood without fear of repercussions and talked about my relationship with Eva, including doubts and hesitations.

I couldn't say his marriage to our mother had not been a happy one, just one with no emotion. He was a stoic Army man who showed no outward affection and our mother was a woman who craved more. But he could not give it and she withered away young, the seemingly loveless union taking years from her. She died when I was in high school. After the funeral was over, friends and family finally gone and just the three of us in our small house, I think we all realized the loss wasn't new. It had happened years earlier but her body had held on. We had to cook our own meals and do laundry, the biggest adjustments from losing her. We each loved her in our own way but had grown prematurely to compensate for what wasn't there. It's probably what made Shelley and me so independent but at the same time connected to each other. I moved out for college as Shelley did two years before me, and neither of us slept another night in the house where we'd spent so many years.

We both rested beside our father's final bed, falling asleep leaning on each other as we had as children watching television late into the night. One of us would twitch and wake the other up, then fall back to sleep again. I woke once and Shelley was standing in the open sliding door, watching a boy climb the monkey bars.

"You okay?"

She nodded. "I miss that age. The kids are so big now. There's no one to cuddle."

"Cuddle them anyway. Steal those moments where you can," I said.

She smiled.

A cloud moved through the otherwise clear sky and for a few moments blocked the sun, sending the playground outside into shades of grey. Once gone it was technicolor again, the boy's brightly colored green and blue shirt vibrant in the sunlight.

Shelley came back in with cups of coffee and gave me one. We sat on the chairs that looked across the bed to the outside and watched the contrast of old and young, living and dying. The sounds of laughter floated through the open door when not drowned out by the air being pushed out of the mask by a grey machine sitting on the bedside table.

"What did his doctor say?"

She scooted her chair closer to mine, the leg scraping against the tile floor, then rested her head on my shoulder. "Not much. Treatment wasn't doing anything and she recommended this place."

"Seems nice here," I said. "Peaceful enough."

"I've been trying to get ahold of you for two weeks, Eddie," she said. "I didn't want to make the decision by myself. I shouldn't have to."

"I'm sorry."

"You should have been with me, helped me."

I thought about explaining why I'd ignored her messages and calls but knew they were just excuses. Nothing could make up for it. She had every right to be mad at me, to hate me for not being there when she needed me most, but instead she was leaning against me, her arms wrapped around mine, as we watched our father dying.

"You tell Eva?"

"Yeah. She wants to come but is stuck at work." I didn't want Shelley to know I had Eva in hiding. Ideally Shelley and her family would have taken a road trip to be out of the area, but if I even brought the topic up again her husband would go crazy. "You know, she's spent more time with him the last year than I have."

"I know. I bumped into her at the nursing home a few times," Shelley said. "Eddie, I like her. I really like her."

I smiled and felt my head warm. "I do too."

"Don't fuck it up."

"I won't."

CHAPTER 29

My phone vibrated and woke me. Shelley's head was leaning on my arm. I saw Gus's name on screen and answered.

"What's up?"

"I'm outside. We need to talk."

Shelley stirred and let me stand. I glanced at the clock. I'd been asleep for at least an hour, maybe more. Our father was in the same position, the sound of the air pushing into him a constant in the room.

Gus was already waiting in front of the hospice center in his black SUV and I climbed in.

"I'm really sorry to bother you."

"It's fine. I can use a break."

"I know what you need." He pulled the SUV out of the parking lot and turned left across traffic.

"How is he?"

"Comfortable is what I'm supposed to say, I think. There isn't much difference from the last several years in the way of interaction, but you can tell he's going. He's just… fading."

"I'm sorry."

Gus had known my dad when we were growing up though we spent most of our time at his house instead of mine. The Ramirez household had music and laughter and there was always great food being served all times of the day and evening. My love of real Mexican food came from his mother and abuela constantly handing me something to try.

A mile down the road he slowed and turned into the Sonic parking lot and parked in one of the open spaces.

"The usual?" he said.

I nodded while staring at nothing out the front window. He placed the order through the small metal speaker and microphone.

"You okay to talk work a little?"

"Of course." I tried to shake myself out of wherever my head was, somewhere between childhood memories and adult regrets.

"Marcus Knowles called."

"The half-pint cowboy?" My curiosity pulled back to the moment. "What did he want?"

"He got a call from Hubble."

"Hubble's in hiding and still makes his pot order?"

"Not exactly. Marcus said he was insisting on a large shipment of Fentanyl."

"Making the jump to the serious drugs. How large a shipment?"

"He wants at least a hundred pounds."

"That would be worth over a million dollars on the street," I said. "Marcus going to get it for him?"

"We talked about that. As a federal agent I can't really allow it to happen but it's also a way to catch Hubble and Ortiz in a solid crime to put them away."

"Let me guess," I said. "Fake shipment?"

"Bingo," Gus said. "Marcus has agreed to help, setting up a truck to look like it came in from Mexico at the right time in case Hubble and Ortiz are watching the border. Then a rendevouz point near here to do the deal."

"Why would he do that?"

"He promised to never touch the hard stuff again. Only marijuana from here on out if we forget about him after this is over."

"That's a limited market nowadays. Before long it's going to be legal everywhere."

"I'm not sure he realizes that," Gus said.

"Why are Hubble and Ortiz switching from pot?" I was talking out loud, mostly to myself.

"My thought is they're looking for a fast infusion of money—"

"To disappear," I finished his thought. "This is probably our last chance to get them."

"We have a few days to plan," Gus said. "It would take a while for an order like that to come together and get here from Mexico."

"But also can't make it seem like Marcus is stalling them," I said. "Guess it's time to place a fake drug order."

Food came and was handed through the window. Our conversations turned from Marcus and Hubble to random thoughts of high school and college. The human brain is a curious thing, bringing up memories thought lost once they are needed. We laughed at the stupid things we'd done, sighed over the rejections from girls asked out, and shook our heads wondering how we were still alive from the way we drove as teenagers.

After ordering a second round of cherry limeades and one for Shelley, Gus dropped me off. He pulled away and I waited until his Explorer turned right and disappeared. I sat on a bench out front of the building. A faded gold plate had the name of some donor who'd gifted it, a small place away from the dying to get your thoughts on other things for a few moments before returning to the bedside.

I wanted to go get Eva. She deserved to see my dad before he died. But I wasn't going to risk it. She'll be there when it is time, to support me when I needed it most. Through the doors of the hospice center the first thing I noticed was crying down the hallway. I almost dropped the two cups to run but as quickly as I'd heard it, I realized the cries were from the nearest patient room. A nurse closed the door as I walked by but not before I saw an elderly woman with her head on the chest of the man lying in bed.

Shelley was sitting up in the chair where I'd left her flipping through a magazine she'd read at least ten times already. When I closed the door behind me she looked up and saw the large white cups in my hands.

"Gimme, gimme!"

I handed her a cup and glanced at our dad. "Any change?"

"No," she said. "He stirred for a moment, like he has for the last year or two, you know."

I knew. When I'd sit with him at the home there were glimpses of something in his eyes that lasted seconds. As quickly as it had come, he was back inside his own head.

Conversation came and went as needed, silence when it was time and laughter when we were ready. We talked about his arrangements. It's a positive side of hospice, if there is one. It brings family together to allow them to decide and finalize everything that needs to happen once your loved one dies. Instead of the rush and pressure of something sudden, you have a few days or even weeks to make sure the funeral is planned and locations are secured. I already knew where to hold the reception and Shelley smiled when I suggested it.

She took her place leaning on my arm again, the silence interrupted every few seconds by the slurping sound from the straw in her styrofoam cup.

"You have to leave, don't you." She didn't say it as a question.

"Yeah."

"When?"

"Soon."

"Is it important?"

"Not as important as this," I said. "But hopefully it will put a couple of bad people away."

"Dad would understand."

"I'm not sure about that."

"Is it dangerous?"

"Yes."

Her arm tightened on mine. "Tell Eva. Don't hide anything from her."

"I'll tell her."

CHAPTER 30

I tapped lightly on the hotel room door. A moment later I saw the peephole go dark. The door opened. She didn't look any more happy with me but still wrapped her arms around my body. I melted into her, feeling her warmth, her hand on the back of my neck. I never wanted to leave that moment.

She kissed me. I kissed her back.

As we moved toward the bed I saw the door to Clem's room was closed. She grabbed the remote and turned up the volume on the television to cover our sounds. I'd made love to things more disturbing than Chip and Joanna Gaines arguing over whether a wall should be moved ten inches. I also suspected Eva wanted to know how the episode ended.

Clothes were left in a trail on the floor and tossed onto the second bed which was serving as her suitcase holder. I've never gotten tired of being with this woman, of her touch, her kiss, her body. She was all I needed and all I wanted.

Skin pressed against skin as lips and tongues moved across each other. For months after we began to date, whenever we were together, made love, I was aware of the fact that each time could be the last time. That at any point she may decide that I wasn't the one she wanted to be with anymore or that being alone was just better than being with someone who put their life in danger so often. But a week turned into a month and now almost three years. We share a bed, a home, our lives. I taught her to shoot, she taught me to not leave my underwear on the floor.

We collapsed into each other, her body wrapped up in mine as my fingers softly stroked her slightly sweaty skin, hers swirling around on my chest. I loved her and and I knew she loved me, which was a first. For several months my thoughts had gone to further out than I'd ever let them, not just what's for dinner tonight, a weekend trip in a month, or a vacation next winter. But years. And I always saw here beside me.

First we talked about my father. I knew she wanted to ask more questions about his health but didn't. She knew it didn't really matter at this point. His shell was giving out, even if his brain was still in there somewhere. She'd pushed to help get him into some experimental research through the university but I resisted it, knowing he wouldn't have wanted to be a footnote in a four hundred page report.

Then I told her everything that had happened with the case and what was still to come. Our plan wasn't complete, still working on the details as much as we could without knowing everything that could go sideways. Gus and I had driven out to where the drug deal would take place and walked every foot of it so we knew where hiding places were and where we'd be most vulnerable. One side was blocked by water. There was only one way in and out.

She listened and said nothing until I was done. There were the few minutes of silence that I knew well, her grinding through the plot until she knew what wasn't fitting.

"They're desperate," she said.

"Most likely."

"No, I mean really desperate. Everything they have is sunk into their house, their cars, their kids."

"What are you getting at?"

"They'll do anything to get away free." She paused as if to process through another thought. "If they think you and Gus are what's in their way, they won't hesitate to kill you."

"Aww, that's sweet, baby."

"Are you not taking this seriously?"

"Of course I am, but I can't stress myself out thinking about it." I'd been in the line of fire more times than she knew about, even since we'd been together. If I let everyone who wanted to kill me get in my head, I'd never leave the house.

"Whatever you do, you two need to be ready to end them before they end you."

"You sure you're a doctor?"

"Yes and I don't want to see you on a bed in my emergency room again," she said. "Or worse."

"But that's how we met."

She tried to hide the smile, turning it quickly to a

grimace that was obviously fake. My hands stretched wide and moved across her flat stomach as my mouth reached hers again and our tongues met. I wanted this woman every day, all day. And luckily, she wanted me, too.

CHAPTER 31

If you are ever preparing for a mission and aren't nervous, it's time to quit. Find a new job. Go into retail. Work for an insurance company. The moment you aren't nervous is when you'll screw up and get either you or someone else on your team dead. Nerves keep you sharp. They make you triple check that your magazine is seated properly and a round is in the chamber. They allow you to hear every sound around you.

My Glock 17 was cleaned and reassembled. A magazine was in with seventeen rounds of jacketed hollow points and one in the chamber. No safety to get in the way. Ready to shoot. My usual cargo shorts were left at home. Lightweight 5.11 TacLite tactical pants were worn in their place along with my Army Rangers T-shirt won off Clem a year earlier. It seemed appropriate since he got us into this shit. I'd have a vest on over the shirt when the time came. Five more magazines were loaded and on my belt.

Eva was at the hotel, Clem in the room next to her. I hadn't asked him but I'm sure he had at least three weapons hidden around the room. She reluctantly had the Glock 26 I'd given her when we moved in together. I'm a romantic.

I heard a horn and checked myself one more time. I set the alarm and locked the house. After climbing into Gus's SUV I saw his Sig Sauer on his side and belt with extra magazines.

"The back loaded?" I said.

He nodded. "Two MP5's with plenty of ammunition, a pair of Remington 870's, two vests, and a case of water."

I looked over at him.

"Gotta stay hydrated," he said.

As we pulled away I glanced in the side view mirror at the house I shared with Eva and made the promise to myself, as I always did, that I would return to it and her. I wanted to promise myself this was the last time I'd leave knowing I might not come back, but knew I couldn't.

"How's backup looking?" I said.

"Slim."

He didn't have to say anymore than that. It was a risky operation complicated by the fact that the primary target was a current Army officer, his wife and partner-in-crime a former Army officer. Then throw in a known drug dealer aiding in the op, and a load of fake drugs. Agencies want slam dunks. They want to know who they are getting, for what crime, and to take immediate credit for the bust. They don't want a clusterfuck in the middle of nowhere to clean up and hope they can make some charges stick.

We didn't talk much after that. Over the years we'd both been in dangerous situations, separately and together. I always felt better when Gus was there, but also hated putting him in danger. I'm sure he felt the same way.

The drive was just under an hour. I never even turned on the stereo to look for some good music. It wasn't the time for it. Maybe on the drive back when we were both alive and had a lot of drinks to look forward to. Hell, I might even let him pick the music, but probably not.

The Pederanales River winds through west Texas for more than a hundred miles before dumping into the Colorado River outside Austin. The dam upriver restricts its flow and in many places you can walk across the flint rock to the other side. We came from the south and turned off Texas State Highway 71 onto a dirt road that goes down to the river, an access point used mainly by weekend fishermen, teens looking for a place to drink and have sex, and now a million dollar drug deal. By the end of the day there would likely be at least one dead body on the dirt. I just hoped it wasn't me.

The access road drops down below the level of the highway for instant privacy from people traveling by at speed and the tree line blocks the view from the other side of the river. The closest houses were a half mile away through thick trees. It was one way in and out and that's what we wanted, a bottleneck to trap them. With more resources, other agencies to back us up to create a proper perimeter, we could have chosen somewhere else.

We circled back up and hit a side trail we'd chosen on our recon trip to the site and drove down in far enough to hide the SUV from view. Vests on, we inspected each other. Guns checked one more time. A couple bottles of water each were put into the large pockets on our pants.

I looked at Gus. "Ready?"

He nodded.

It was a short walk and we found our cluster of trees and took shelter. Water bottles were offloaded to the ground so they didn't get in our way if we had to run or fight.

Then it was time for the wait. We kept to ourselves though only a few feet apart. Every movement was thought through over and over, from the muscle memory instinct of pulling our weapons to moving along the tree line swiftly to take the target down. We'd spent all day and most of the night going through the details.

The morning moved easily. We could relax as long as one of us was alert at a time. I had my eyes closed and allowed my thoughts to drift from offensive maneuvers and self defense to Eva for a moment. Then Gus brought me back to reality.

"Two vehicles coming our way," he said. "White Cadillac and a green Ford pickup."

I glanced at him. "Sounds like Marcus is here."

"I'm gonna try to get a selfie with him this time."

"I don't blame you."

I could hear the low rumble of the Caddie as it passed our location. The windows were rolled up and tinted so I couldn't see Marcus. I glanced at my watch. Fifteen minutes until the meet time, but if they were smart—

"Two more vehicles coming down," Gus said. "Black Suburban, tinted windows. No head count. And Hubble's white Honda Pilot, two people inside."

The end of the dirt access road was barely wide enough for two vehicles. The Cadillac and green Ford pickup sat side-by-side facing the rocky hill down to the river. Hubble's two SUV's had them blocked in. It was a tactical weakness that we'd predicted. Hubble and Ortiz being military, we expected them to arrive last and had likely inspected the area through satellite imagery online or even driven out to the location as we had.

There was the momentary stalemate of who would exit their vehicle first when the doors to the Suburban opened. Two men got out. They wore dark street clothes with light jackets that didn't do much to conceal the bulge of the weapons they wore on their belts. They looked ex-military. Hubble and Ortiz stepped out of the Pilot.

"There's the happy couple," Gus said.

The driver of the Cadillac got out and opened the back door. The white Stetson appeared above the door. Marcus Knowles came into sight as he stepped around to the back of his car. His right hand was in its usual position, hovering out from the oversized silver revolver.

"He does not disappoint," I said.

"I'm definitely getting a selfie with him," Gus said.

One man climbed out of the old Ford pickup that had pulled in with him. Gus and I glanced at each other.

"He brought Buck," Gus said.

"And I think he has the same OP shirt on under Sam's Club kevlar."

"It's probably his lucky shirt."

"Worked out so well for him last time we met," I said.

"Wanna bet it's his buddy Jerry with him?"

The other door of the truck opened and a skinny man in faded blue jeans stepped to the ground.

"Yup. It's Jerry," I said. "Looks like they had a two-for-one on vests."

"So Hubble brought two ex-military shooters, along with himself and his wife, both military," Gus said. "And Marcus brought his chauffeur and two idiots who couldn't even tie each other's shoes."

"That's why they both wear boots," I said.

The two shooters had empty hands, showing no sign of feeling threatened. True professionals know when to posture and when to play it cool.

Ortiz and Hubble approached a waiting Marcus and stopped ten feet short of him.

"It's go-time," I said.

CHAPTER 32

Hubble's shooters constantly scanned the perimeter. We stepped behind the nearest trees just to be safe. Hubble and Ortiz followed Marcus and his driver to the back of the pickup. They stood for a moment until Ortiz motioned to the vehicle. Marcus then waved at his driver to open the tailgate.

"Poor Marcus can't do anything for himself," Gus said.

"You can give him a hug later," I said. "This should be it. They just need to move the drugs to the SUVs."

With a glance over his shoulder, Hubble signaled his other shooter to bring a duffel bag from the Suburban. He stepped past his boss and dropped it on the ground. Marcus looked at the bag. His chauffeur knelt down and opened it, Marcus over his shoulder.

In that moment that the two were distracted by the

money, the shooters pulled weapons in fast, smooth motions. Two pairs of suppressed shots were fired before we knew what had happened and Buck and Jerry fell to the ground beside the pickup.

We didn't speak. We didn't have to. Our guns were out and we were in motion. Putting distance between each other, we ran, weapons raised. The two shooters heard us and turned. Gus fired first and I heard the thud of a .40 caliber slug hitting a military grade vest. The man stumbled, but his gun continued to move toward us. Gus fired again and the man's face disappeared, the spent body falling to the side.

I had moved left to draw the other shooter's fire away from Gus. I heard the click of the hammer on his weapon. A half-second later the bullet fired out at me and missed, aim having dropped in the moment before the bullet came out. The man looked at his gun in confusion and I shot him in the left leg. From the ground he acquired his target and fired at me again, missing close to my left. Another click, a delay, then the explosion of the gunpowder from the faulty ammuntion. I felt the bullet hit the ground beside me. I aimed and took my shot. Both of the shooters were dead.

Gus was already moving for Hubble and Ortiz. I went left to flank. The two had taken cover in front of the pickup. Even in Texas, the sound of multiple gunshots would startle people and the police had likely already been called by one of the homes on the other side of the trees or across the river. The only problem with cops showing up is they don't know the good guys from the bad guys.

A shot blasted from a big gun, a .45 I guessed, and came too close too me. I dove left behind the Cadillac. Gus was already there trying to get an angle around the back of the large car. Marcus and his chauffeur were huddled up over the duffel bag, fully exposed.

"Let's end this now, Hubble," I yelled. "Weapons down, hands up."

Another bullet skipped past me. He was shooting below the cars. The next round hit the front tire on the far side and it exploded. One wrong shot and the gas tank would take us all out. I moved forward to block his view with the front left tire of the Caddie.

Then the shots came fast, but nothing was hitting near me.

I turned to Gus. "It's cover fire."

I popped my head up and came back down quickly after looking through the windows of the Cadillac. Even with the tinting I could tell that Ortiz had made it to the cab of the pickup and Hubble was shooting to keep us from seeing. With a hand signal I told Gus to cover me after a silent three count. He was up and shooting over the trunk and Hubble's fire stopped as he ducked. I came out from around the front of the car. Gus would pull his fire up to keep from hitting me. I stopped and had my Glock aimed at Hubble who was cowering on the ground.

"It's over, Hubble," I said. "Throw your weapon away."

His hand still rested on the grip of the .45 in the dirt. My finger put pressure on the trigger in case he moved to shoot. Then his hand released and grabbed the barrel to slide it away.

The blast was loud and close and struck me dead center

in the chest. As I flew backward I saw Ortiz with a pistol pointed out the driver's window of the green pickup. In the moment of remarkable clarity, shot in the chest and flying backward, I saw Ortiz clearly. Her shoulder length brown hair was pulled back in a tight ponytail and she wore no makeup. The faded green pickup had a dented fender and possibly as much rust as paint. Just under the driver's window, with cheap stick on letters, were the words BUCK TRUCK. I hit the ground on my back and couldn't move, only the wide Texas sky in my view. I gasped to catch a breath. I'd been hit in the vest before, but never from ten feet away with that large a caliber.

I'd let myself lose a target. Once again I'd underestimated Leocadia Ortiz and again I ended up bested, this time maybe for good. My heartbeat was loud in my ears, fast and thunderous.

Gunshots sounded around me but I couldn't see, lying like a turtle on its shell, unable to move or defend myself. My gun wasn't in my hand anymore but I wouldn't be able to target anyone if I still had it.

An engine roared to life. It sounded like it was far away. I focused and realized it was the pickup beside me. More gunshots. I heard Gus yelling but couldn't decipher the words. Bullets hit metal.

The pickup took off forward, blocked from heading to the highway by the Suburban and Pilot. The shadow of the truck passed me and the sound faded while being joined by crunches of rocks and more gunfire. Then Gus was over me, his gun still raised and shooting. A magazine flew out to the side with the flick of his wrist, a dry-fire drill we'd practiced hundreds of times, and another put in its place. It was an angle I'd never seen and it was mesmerizing. The brass was flying out the side of his Sig Sauer, red flashes from the muzzle.

Then silence and he was on his knees beside me.

"You okay, buddy?"

I couldn't talk at first, the weight on my chest still heavy. It was hot and constricting.

His hands went to my sides and released the heavy vest. He flipped it over my head. By the look on his face I knew he was relieved.

"You're gonna be sore as hell, but you should live," he said.

I controlled my breath and managed a reply. "Not sure I want to."

"Can you get up?"

I thought about it then nodded. Just having the vest off made me feel better. He grabbed my arms and dead lifted me until I was vertical. The pain was worse than any I'd felt before and I'd actually had bullets enter my body, not just impact on the surface. Bulletproof vests are great that they stop most projectiles, but what people don't realize who've never been shot in one, is they disperse that energy to a wider area. So instead of a bullet hole, you have bruised and broken ribs.

I glanced down at the vest and saw the bulge of the bullet where it had been stopped by the Class IV body armor. The flattened lead from a .45 was sticking out through the black mesh. The ceramic plate was rated for even higher velocity rifle fire but the close range pistol was still no match. I could tell there was at least some broken ribs, the small price to pay for not having a slug in your chest. As much as I needed it on, I couldn't stand the thought of strapping it back around me with the pain throbbing through my body.

"They haven't made it far," Gus said. "I'm going after them."

"Not without me." I looked around for my Glock and couldn't find it.

Behind the Cadillac, Marcus and his chauffeur were still petrified on the ground.

"Stay here with the money. We'll be back for you," Gus said.

Marcus raised his hand and let a wad of cut up newspaper loose in the breeze.

"I do believe they never intended to make good on their side of the transaction," Marcus said.

"Even in misery he still uses too many words," I said.

One of the dead shooters was beside the Suburban. I reached down and took the pistol out of his hand and checked the magazine. It was a suppressed grey bodied CZ 75. At least a dozen rounds left. Gus got in the driver's seat of the SUV and I strapped in beside him.

The Suburban wasn't designed for heavy off road travel but it was a one way trip and didn't belong to us. Gus took off and we followed the track Ortiz had taken down the steep hill toward the Pedernales. It was only a minute until we had eyes on them. The pickup was rear wheel drive and with a mostly empty bed was slipping in the soft mud on the side of the river.

The overweight Suburban flew down the hill and Gus slammed on the brakes, sending my chest into the seatbelt.

"Shit that hurts," I yelled.

"Sorry."

He cranked the wheel left and cut the angle across the brush and weeds then pushed the pedal down. The four wheel drive and was keeping the heavy SUV above the mud and the big V8 had us moving fast.

"He'll have to make a left and try to get to a road eventually," Gus said.

We were catching up to the underpowered pickup while flying down the edge of the river. We passed boathouses and docks on our left that once floated on the water but now rested on the soft ground, waiting for rains to bring the river's level up again. The back of the pickup slid left and the truck spun around facing us then turned and tried to speed away again. We closed the distance to a few car lengths.

The pickup moved up the bank into the grass.

"She's looking for a way through," I said.

"Doesn't have much further to go," Gus said.

Up ahead the soft muddy shore of the river turned to steep rock. Even if they made it up the first one, the flint would shred the balding tires quickly. The pickup made a sharp left between two boathouses and Gus followed, the SUV held better traction, working up to twenty feet off the back of the truck.

The tree line ahead was solid, no trails or roads except for footpaths to the homes the boathouses belonged to, not wide enough for a full size vehicle.

"There's nowhere to go," I said.

I'd barely gotten the words out when the pickup made a sharp right. Gus tried to turn into it to hit the pickup broadside but missed. He cranked the wheel and got back on the gas.

"She's going for the river," I said.

With the pistol taken from one of the dead shooters, I aimed out the window and pulled the trigger.

Click. Nothing. I held the gun steady, then the bullet shot.

"What the hell, was that a hangfire?" Gus said. "What kind of ammo is in that thing?"

The pickup didn't slow and hit the water ahead of us at full speed, plumes flared up from either side. Water and mud hit our windshield. Gus cranked the wheel to get out of the spray while finding the right control for the wipers. Once the blades swept across the windshield we saw the pickup in the middle of the river, the back end moving sideways instead of forward.

"They're bogged down," I said.

Gus angled in through the water to hit them on the right side when Hubble fired out the passenger window at us. We turned sharp and the front of the Suburban sunk into a deeper part of the river. I looked over my shoulder.

"They're free," I said. The pickup found traction and was slowly moving out of the water, the old engine working hard for every inch of forward motion.

I climbed out the window of the SUV, the water now just below the opening, and worked my way to the hood. My chest was in pain but I couldn't just stop.

"Where the hell are you going?" Gus yelled.

The pickup hit the far bank of the river and started up the rocks toward a rutted rocky trail that disappeared into the trees.

"That way." I pointed and jumped off the front of the Suburban into the Pedernales River.

CHAPTER 33

The slow moving water was chest high. My walking was restricted so I did a half doggie paddle, my chest hurting too much to all out swim, until it got shallower. I heard the splash behind me and knew Gus was following.

I hit the far shore and took off running as well as I could. Every breath and movement burned. I knew there were a few broken ribs, probably more damage than that. Gus was catching up to me. The sound of rocks beneath his feet got gradually louder.

It was five minutes up the trail when I first heard it. I stopped running to listen and turned to Gus who was right behind me.

"It's the pickup," he said.

"Sounds like it's stuck again."

Invigorated, we ran hard. The trail was rough, meant for

an all terrain vehicle rather than a thirty year old pickup or an injured runner. We kept to opposite sides near the trees for cover.

The sound of the engine got louder as it revved up, then crunching and more revs.

We paused behind trees and looked ahead. The rear transaxle rested on a large rock in the middle of the trail. The left rear tire still touched the ground, but not enough for traction. The acrid smell of burning rubber was in the air. Hubble was out and trying to push from the back while Ortiz kept gunning the gas. With all the noise they never heard us come up behind them.

The distance was closed to twenty feet before we heard the yell. Ortiz had spotted me in her rear view mirror and Hubble stopped pushing to step to the side of the truck to hear what she was saying. He was unarmed.

"Face down on the ground," I yelled. The gun I'd taken from the dead shooter was in my hands and aimed at him.

His body jerked at my voice and as he turned his foot caught a rock and he went down hard, his head hitting the steel bumper. My aim moved to the cab. With the rear of the truck high-centered, the window line of the door was at eye level. I couldn't see Ortiz.

"Okay, Ortiz. It's over." I moved slowly, never letting my aim drop. I stayed even with the bed of the truck behind the cab in hopes that if she began firing through he metal door she would expect me to be straight out headed for the handle. Once close enough I stretched and looked into the cab and didn't see her. My hand went to the rusty chrome handle and pushed the button with my thumb to open the door.

The idling engine screamed to life and I yanked the door open. Ortiz was on the floorboard, one hand on the gas pedal, the other pulling down the gearshift on the column. In the moment before I understood what was about to happen, the gearshift moved and the transmission dropped into reverse. The tire that had no traction to move forward up the hill caught with the change in direction with the assistance of gravity, and the truck hopped off the rock. With the sudden backward and downhill momentum, the door flew all the way open and caught me broadside as the pickup went down the hill. My left arm reached out and grabbed the window frame, my feet dragged the ground as we accelerated, Ortiz still pushing the gas pedal down. The rocky surface jammed my legs under the door, continually crushing my knees and shins into the bottom edge of the metal.

A crunch and groan and I looked left through the open window to see Hubble after both left tires went over his legs. I pulled my feet up during a gap in the rocks and got them onto the floorboard then flung my body in, kicking Ortiz in the chest, sending her backward. The truck was moving fast and bouncing around. With no one steering, it jerked left and right. A last view out the windshield I saw Gus running to Hubble's limp body.

Ortiz came at me, hands out to punch or claw or push me back out the door. I brought the pistol up to Ortiz's head. She paused. I pulled the trigger.

Her body stiffened with the click. In the absence of an immediate bullet, her hand pushed my arm toward the front of the truck. The bullet fired, a quarter sized hole appeared in the windshield which quickly spider-webbed and the gun fell to my left onto the floor in the mess of fast food bags and cracked CD cases. She pushed up from her position on the floor and tried to drive me back out the still open door. My left arm looped through the steering wheel which kept me from flying backward but also steadied the path of the pickup, allowing it to gain more speed.

Her fist hit my chest dead center where she'd shot me in the vest and the pain renewed. All the air left my lungs faster than a popped ballon. A bump brought the door slamming into the top of my head. She reached over me, a knee coming into my groin, and caught the handle, slamming the door into my head two more times. I brought my legs up and worked to push her back, but she got on top of me again and came at my face, fingers out. I caught her hair with my right hand before she gouged my eyes and slammed her face into the steering wheel, the horn letting out a sharp honk with each strike.

With her scraping at my right arm as I held her back, I let loose of the steering wheel with my left elbow and felt down to the floor until it found the barrel of the gun. I spun it in place and brought it up wrong handed and shoved the muzzle into her neck. I felt her body tense as we made eye contact. Any hesitation I thought I might have to shoot a woman was gone. It was her or me.

I pulled the trigger.

Click.

We both paused, waiting for the blast of the .40 caliber, the gun still in her throat. Did she know what I did, that the ammo was bad? The moment hung longer than it really lasted, milliseconds seemed like minutes.

Her hand grabbed my arm and pushed it toward the windshield so the bullet wouldn't hit her if it fired. I let go of her hair with my right hand and as she pushed it away, I grabbed the slide on the semi-automatic pistol and pulled it back hard. The misfired shell ejected, hitting her skin just above the collar of her shirt and got caught in the material. As her hands left me to search for it, I twisted left. My momentum took me to the floorboard.

The faulty primer inside the cartridge finally hit the powder with a delayed reaction and the round exploded. The blast only had a radius of a couple of feet, but inside the pickup cab, I felt shrapnel hit my back. The truck still bounced down the trail, slowing as the hill turned to flat near the river. I grabbed the steering wheel to help me up and turned to look at her.

Leocadia Ortiz was leaned back against the passenger door, hands held to her throat. Blood flowed between her fingers. Her eyes looked at me and as she tried to speak, bubbles of blood formed on her lips. I lunged forward and applied pressure, knowing it would do no good.

She was looking at me when she died. Her body gave out. The flow of blood stopped once her heart was no longer pumping. Her eyes didn't close. I reached out, the pain almost stopping me, and lowered her eyelids.

I leaned back against the steering wheel and looked out at the Padernales River, the back of the truck sitting in the water. The engine had died and I could hear the flow of water a few feet away, moving around the tires on its endless journey.

My chest burned with each breath and I felt I might end up dead beside her in the cab of the Buck Truck. Not the death I expected for myself. I always imagined something slightly more humorous. A death that people would not want to talk about at first because it was so embarrassing, but over time it became something nobody would believe and laugh about over drinks and memories of me. I don't think Ortiz thought she'd die like this, either. She had three children somewhere waiting for her, but her end was the result of her own actions.

I'm not leaving anything behind except sadness from my few friends and family along with boxes of concert T-shirts that hadn't been opened in a couple years stacked up in a garage. I reached up and touched my face, fingers bringing back a thick red liquid. I smelled it then touched it to my tongue. Ketchup. Of course. Maybe that's the story they'll tell. Eddie Holland died in a dirty pickup truck in the Pedernales River with ketchup from a half eaten fast food burger all over his face. It's not perfect, but it will have to do.

The sound of the water got louder but I couldn't sit up to look out the window anymore. My eyes closed and the words to an old Guy Clark song entered my mind and wouldn't leave. My mouth moved but no sound came out as I sang the words about an old man dying as he pondered if anything he'd done in his life had lasted.

The river grew louder and more violent around me, shaking the truck as I went unconscious.

CHAPTER 34

In law enforcement, taking a life is never the goal in a mission. Leocadia Ortiz didn't deserve to die. She didn't need to die. The two shooters she brought with her didn't either. But when it comes down to me or someone else, I will always pick me. Call me selfish.

Police and FBI would much rather have someone go through the court system and receive their sentence. We didn't sign up to be judge and jury. A body count is never gloated and not something we ever want to deal with alone in the darkness once the shooting is over and we just need to sleep. Too many good officers and agents have lost their edge from the mental trauma and were never able to carry a badge and gun again. I'd killed several men in the line of duty and in self defense, and now one woman. I had trouble sleeping after the first one. Never again since. I came to terms with their deaths and my living.

I'd step in front of a bullet for Eva. Or a truck or a train. That was something I'd realized in the cab of that pickup with someone else's blood all over me and a concussion forcing me in and out of consciousness.

I was stirred awake by a rumbling sound, then the pickup shook and dirt flew up all around and in through the broken windows. The Texas Sate Police helicopter landed on the soft bank of the Pedernales not far from where the pickup had eventually rolled to a stop. Commands were shouted but I couldn't respond, instead blacking out once more.

The helicopter was airborne when my eyes opened again. I was strapped to a stretcher, arms immobile, a neck brace on and a mask over my nose and mouth. A needle was in my arm and I felt the warmth from whatever was flowing into my blood. My mind raced with the sudden inhalation of pure oxygen. Images flashed through my subconscious, as clear as if they were in front of me. Eva. Gus. Clem. Ortiz dying in a pickup beside me. Then older memories and tragedies. Buddy dead on the floor of the bar, the assassin Aran Driscoll over him with a gun. Peter Miller bleeding to death in an FBI safe house. I snapped my eyes open again only to have a bright flashlight shining in to check my dilation.

"Can you hear me?" The voice was stern but somehow caring.

I tried to nod but the neck brace and strap across my forehead didn't allow it. I blinked instead.

"Good," the medic said. "You likely have a concussion and possibly internal bleeding. We're on our way to the closest hospital."

I blinked my eyes rapidly to get his attention and he removed my mask for a moment. I was able to force out a single word. He put the mask back on me and spoke into the mic on his headset then nodded.

"Memorial is only a few minutes farther," he said. "We can do that."

My eyes closed again. I don't know if I slept, was knocked out by painkillers, or simply passed out from my injuries. Images appeared again, but of my dad. I saw him young and healthy when Shelley and I were children, passing through the room without a word as we played. He sat at the end of the small kitchen table at dinnertime in the little house his Army salary could afford, utensils in hand and eating as if it were only a need, mechanical actions of cutting and chewing until he was finished. In each scene that played out, the focus changed from the memories I'd always had, the years of thinking of him as uncaring and disconnected from me and Shelley. Instead I saw as he walked past us on the floor, toys spread out in active play. At the dinner table, food on our plates and leftovers to last days. Mom kissing our foreheads at bedtime, Dad already asleep to be ready for another long day of work. Warm blankets pulled up to our necks.

Eva was beside the hospital bed when I woke, flipping through the pages of my report.

"Hello, Dr. Taylor," I said.

She looked up at me and tried to hide her smile.

"Mr. Holland," she said.

"Am I gonna live?"

"You have a concussion, but will survive it, yes. You also

have three broken ribs and a sucking chest wound."

"Am I able to do any physical labor or exercise?"

"No."

"What about running?"

"I wouldn't recommend it." She let her smile come out as she realized what was happening.

"Mountain climbing?"

We'd first met when I was in the emergency room of this hospital. She gave me the MRI report on my head injury and we'd had this same conversation.

"Definitely not," she said.

"Quiet dinner for two?"

She took my hand. "That would be fine."

"Great. Every night for the rest of your life?"

Her head tilted, eyes opened wide. "Excuse me?"

The door to my room opened before I could continue. Gus appeared first then held the door for Shelley and Clem. My sister was at the bed in two steps and I could tell she didn't know whether to punch me or hug me. She settled for gently kissing me on the forehead. I could see she needed to talk, her nervous glance around the room at everyone else then back to me. I exhaled slowly and looked at the ceiling for a moment then back to her face. There was only one thing it could be.

"I know," I said.

She tilted her head. "Who told you?"

"No one. I can just read you."

Her body leaned over and hugged me. The pressure on my chest hurt but I didn't say anything.

"When?" I said.

"Last night."

I gave a slight nod. "Peaceful?"

"As much as he ever was."

I felt a tear begin to form in my right eye, the first I would ever have for my father. Through yelling and fights, a year of not talking after high school when I chose college instead of the Army, then his Alzheimer's diagnosis and years in the nursing home, my feelings for him never changed. He was my father but I loved him in a distant way. I often wondered if it were the same for him, or if Shelley and I were just bumps on his road, another mission to take on and complete. He was an Army man. He didn't show emotion, he didn't profess his love. Those were signs of weakness and the one thing a military man always fears is looking weak. But now, in his death, I felt it had always been more than that. We were well cared for. We had food on the table and toys to play with. Our backpacks always had paper and pencils and plenty of books to read. He had completed his mission. He'd prepared us.

CHAPTER 35

I sat in a booth at Buddy's Music Parlor to celebrate another life, just as we had the night Gus and I decided to buy the bar during the memorial for Buddy. Again, Gus was across from me beside Shelley and Eva was at my side, connected to me. The addition this time was Clem at the end of the table. There were people on stage, though not music this time as it had been for Buddy. A stream of retired Army men were talking about our father in ways we'd never thought of him. Stories of practical jokes and funny moments, acts of bravery and once slipping in a mud puddle resulting in a young woman coming to his aid as his friends stood and laughed. It was a story I'd heard from our mother many times, possibly her effort to humanize an emotionless father.

"Eddie, Gus, I don't know how to thank you enough," Clem said.

We shook our heads. "You don't have to," Gus said.

"You would have done the same for us," I said.

Clem put his hand on my shoulder.

Gus looked at his watch. "Leocadia Ortiz's funeral is happening right now."

It had only been five days since we took her down. I'd spent four of those in the hospital and last night back at home with Eva. Gus had been left to clean up the mess at the Pedernales.

"Wonder what kind of turn out she'll get," I said, not unkindly.

"After what she's done, can't imagine much," Clem said. "Soldiers are family until they are betrayed."

"Hubble got a special release to go, though. They don't consider him much of a flight risk right now," Gus said.

"Yeah. Hubble is hobbled," I said. "Guess he's going to be in a wheelchair for a long time after getting run over by his wife."

"He still has a dozen agents attending with him. He might not be able to run off, but they didn't want to take any chance that any of his men would come take him," Gus said. "Army JAG is letting FBI have him first while they do a full investigation in their ranks of who Ortiz had in her pocket. More than a few stripes are going to be lost over this."

I looked up at Gus. "What ever happened with Marcus Knowles and his guys?"

"State police had Marcus and his driver locked up for two days before I could get enough pressure from above to let them go. I made him a promise and I had to keep it.

Buck and Jerry took hard hits to their box store vests but are okay. A few broken ribs between them. They're probably back home now in whatever trailer park they live in."

"Good to hear," I said.

Gus took his phone from his jacket pocket and tapped it a few times. "Best part is this, though."

He turned the phone so I could see the large screen. A smiling Gus was kneeling down with his arm around a very unamused Marcus Knowles.

"You got your selfie!" I said.

"Told him I'd forget our deal if he didn't do it," he said. "William Jennings came forward on his own. He had told his wife everything and decided to do the right thing. Looks like he'll get leniency for providing his testimony against Hubble and Ortiz. No jail time. Same for Hector Santos. The feds are good with him, but the Army is investigating whether he should be disciplined. He's also getting therapy after the suicide threat."

"If there's anything I can do to help," I said.

"Same here," Clem said. "I'll talk to some people I know, see what can be done. He was a good soldier."

Our father's funeral was to be small, but the local American Legion had come out in full strength to show respect for a fallen soldier. A 21-gun salute followed a short but sincere sermon by the preacher that regularly visited the nursing home and had probably sat with my father more than I had.

A young man was on stage, his left arm missing inside the poorly fitting uniform he wore. He never knew my father but spoke about the brotherhood of serving and showing respect. As he finished I got up and went to the stage, unplanned and unprepared.

Though I didn't know most of the people in the room, they all knew I was Ed Holland's son. They had come to the bar after the funeral at my invitation. I had an open bar but the tip jars were overflowing.

I stood at the microphone, the one place I'd never been at in my own bar, and looked out at the faces.

"I'm humbled listening to you all speak today," I said. "It seems so many of you knew my father better than I ever did, even those of you that never met him."

I glanced over at the booth where Eva, Gus, Clem, and Shelley sat, their eyes all open wide at my unlikely appearance on stage.

"My family is smaller than it was a few days ago." I looked above the crowd, avoiding eye contact as the emotion of the moment hit me. "Thanks to all of you, though, I feel part of a bigger family right now. I didn't spend as much time with my father as I should have the last few years. I have a lot of excuses, each as worthless as the last."

Heads nodded in understanding.

"And I'm not going to preach to you, tell you to pick up the phone and make that call you haven't made in too long, or drive down to the nursing home only a few miles away. I didn't do it often enough and have no right to tell anyone else to. But I will say this, that I'm not going to let those close to me, the people that I love, slip away as my father did."

My eyes moistened and I knew I had to get off stage.

"So stay as long as you like. Tell stories and lies about

Ed Holland to each other. And drink up until we run out."

I had never heard clapping as I left a stage, it wasn't a situation I was ever meant to be in. Hands slapped my back as I worked my way to my seat.

"What?" I said. Everyone around my table was staring at me.

"Who the hell are you?" Gus said.

"I'm Eddie Holland." I raised my beer bottle. "Son of Ed. Brother of Shelley. Friend of Gus and Clem. Lover of Eva."

They raised their bottles and glasses, clinked them together, and we drank.

We watched the revelry around us as the veterans and active duty soldiers drank and cheered each other. People stopped by our table to offer condolences on our father and thanks for the drinks. Nobody looked sad and there was a lot of laughter in the room.

I looked over at Eva. Her eyes staring back made me smile. I wanted to speak, but didn't, couldn't.

"I know," she said.

"What?"

"I know what you want to say."

"Do you?"

"Yes."

"How?"

"I can just read you."

I smiled.

"Will you?" I said.

"I will."

CHAPTER 36

Three months later

A single bare bulb on a pole sat on the stage, casting a hard light across the room. The high top tables and stools created long shadows that reached toward the bar with an Escher-like quality. It was quiet and smelled like freshly mopped floors with a hint of stale beer resting above it.

I sat alone at the bar, sipping a Shiner Bock while going through receipts and cash. Most nights my manager did this, perks of being the owner, but I let him and the waitresses go home after a particularly lively crowd and concert. Money was counted and in the heavy deposit bag. I put it in the safe under the bar and spun the dial to lock it for the night. Vic would take it to the bank in the morning.

My ribs were healed but still sore at times. I'd had three broken, a sucking chest wound, and more bruises than I cared to count. But I was running, working out, and getting stronger than I had been. I owed it to myself and to Eva. At least one morning a week I went to the shooting range, honing my skills further, and had even been working with a trainer I knew from Austin SWAT. Just because I was getting older didn't mean I couldn't get better.

It was still hot outside even though it was 2:30 in the morning. Eva was working the night shift and I thought about grabbing some food and taking it to her. It was self-serving as I just wanted to see her. I always wanted to see her.

I locked the front door of the bar and turned to look at my car. The pickup hadn't been worth the cost of fixing, so I'd donated it to a high school auto shop and had been switching rental cars out every few weeks. That week was a base model Toyota Camry. I wanted another old VW. I'd missed my Karmann Ghia since the moment it was destroyed during a case over a year earlier and decided that I would find another one, or something similar.

The remote unlocked the door to the Camry as I walked around the car. I stopped. The hair on my neck stood on end. My first thought was that my Glock was in the safe back at home, then I felt silly for immediately going to a life or death situation.

I grabbed the door handle and paused when I saw the movement on the other side of the car. A shadow shifted from just beside the front door of the bar. Whoever it was, I'd walked right past them. I'd stood there, locking the door, inches away from the ghosted figure.

The shadow came toward me, out of the darkness of the awning over the front of the building until the street light illuminated the shape. The figure was shorter than me by a couple of inches, and slender. The head was covered by the dark hood of a jacket, but I knew who it was. I'd thought several times about this man over the last few months and had figured he'd disappeared, gone off to find someone else to fight for after Leocadia Ortiz died.

The only skin I could see were his hands. In one was the blade that had left two scars on my back.

I stared at where his eyes would be, hidden in the blackness inside the hood, and wondered if this was his true being, if I was seeing who he really was. A shadow. If he was here to kill me, I wasn't sure I could stop him. I was getting stronger, but I knew his speed and accuracy. If he'd wanted to kill me the first time we met, I would have been dead.

We stood in silence for several minutes, a stalemate across a beige Camry. When he finally spoke, his voice came softly through the early morning air. It traveled easily, though was said with little force.

"You know who I am?"

I nodded. "You're the Nepali."

"Do you know why I'm here?"

"Honestly, I don't. Your boss is dead, so you aren't getting paid anymore."

"I do not care about money," he said. "I care about honor, about defending the name of my master."

"Your master? Honor? Leocadia Ortiz was a common criminal. You may not care, but she stole from her own country and she had people killed to protect herself."

"I did not serve that woman. She was weak and selfish."

"Then who do you serve?"

"The true master. The one that brings harmony. The Ruby rising in the east."

"Right," I said. "That all made total sense."

"You mock what you do not understand. You are as simple and weak as the woman was."

"Maybe. But she's dead and I'm alive, so there's that."

"She was meant to die that day, you were not. Your abilities are meaningless."

"What about today? Am I meant to die today?"

He paused too long and for a moment I worried.

"No, you are not."

"Then why are you here? Just out for a late night stroll?" I said. "Have you checked out the bats at sunset? You really should, they're quite—"

"You live today, Mr. Holland." The Nepali's soft voice somehow came over the top of mine. "But do not come for the Ruby or I will decide your day."

He moved back into the shadow, his slight frame disappearing before me.

"That's it? You're just going to threaten me and step back into the dark corner?"

There was no answer.

"Hello? Scary dude? You there?"

I got in the car, keeping my eyes on the area under the awning, never letting them drop as I found the ignition and turned the car on. Putting the transmission in reverse, I turned the wheel and backed out into the middle of 6th Street, the headlights of the Camry casting across the front of the buildings until they landed on the front of my bar.

The Nepali was gone.

ABOUT THE AUTHOR

I hate writing these things. They're supposed to read like the author didn't write them, like "John H. Matthews lives in the Washington D.C. suburbs of Virginia with his wife and son." That's silly. Of course I'm writing this.

So, I do live in the Washington D.C. suburbs of Northern Virginia with my wife and son. I write between drives to take my boy to one of many soccer practices and games a week.

Writing is something I do because I love it, it's fun and creative and allows me to go anywhere in the world through my characters, and because I get to sit down while doing it.

The first serious thing I wrote that I kept was a short story while living in Northern California. I was reading all of John Steinbeck's novels again and felt inspired.

My writing heroes are John Steinbeck, Babara Kingsolver, and S.E. Hinton. Is that enough about me?

THANKS

Special thanks to Shea Megale for editing the novel for me. She is an incredibly talented writer (author of *This is Not a Love Scene*, available now, and *American Boy*, coming soon.)

Thank you to my beta readers, those who get to see a book before it publishes and provide valuable feedback, catch plot holes and find tuypoes.. My beta readers: Edward Hutchison, Steve Fox, and June Lane.

My writer's group, the Writers of Chantilly, is a great group of people that provide feedback and inspiration. If you want to be a writer, then start writing and join a writer's group.

And, as cheesy as it sounds, thank you to my readers. The support and love for Eddie Holland has always kept me going.